WARLOCK'S
GIFT

WARLOCK'S GIFT

ARDATH MAYHAR

DOUBLEDAY & COMPANY, INC.
GARDEN CITY, NEW YORK
1982

All of the characters in this book
are fictitious, and any resemblance
to actual persons, living or dead,
is purely coincidental.

Dedicated to Miss Bea, the best postmaster in the business

Library of Congress Cataloging in Publication Data

Mayhar, Ardath.
Warlock's gift.

I. Title.
PS3563.A962W3   813'.54
AACR2
ISBN 0-385-17359-8
Library of Congress Catalog Card Number 81–43149

First Edition

Prelude
THE CITY IN THE PLAIN

Varil's face was warmed to amber by the firelight. Her bright hair was a blaze, in itself, as it curled vigorously upward from her wide forehead. The frown of concentration between her brows did nothing to lessen the loveliness of her tranquil proportions, yet the closed eyes hid such striving as she had never before attempted.

Even as she thrust her skill and her will against the fabric of time, she was aware of the night outside her warm room. In that night that stretched away over Lantirion existed those she loved and those she feared and dreadfully mistrusted. Into that blackness an unnatural snow was beginning to fall, and she knew that she must succeed, now, or she and her land and all whom she loved might well perish in that bitter chill.

The city lay in the loop of the pale blue river. It was patterned like a pendant—a pendant made of topaz and rosy stone—and its shape was as inevitable as the flow of the land about it or of the river which formed one arc of its circle. It was a work of great skill wedded to even greater art, for each house was individually itself, yet all melded together into such completeness as is seldom found in the workings of men.

The central stone of the brooch that was Venelantir was also its highest point, as well as being its most elaborate structure. The Palace of Ven was faceted. Six in-ward-slanted tiers soared upward from the lushly planted courtyard, and each was encircled by a balcony that touched at the six angles and curved free of the planes. The balconies were of gold-colored metal, unornamented. The free-soaring elegance of their design made the entire palace seem to be on the point of rising quietly into the air.

The notion pleased Allitra greatly. As her own bulk in-creased with the growing child, she often dreamed of the unburdened youth that she had so recently left behind. The feeling of lightness and motion that she could regain as she gazed downward from her own balcony, the highest of all, gave her a little ease from the weariness of her pres-ent condition.

It also eased her loneliness. A bit. A tiny bit. For Kereno, Lord of Ven, was dead. If she had, at first, resented her pregnancy, with Kereno's death that had ended. Within her she preserved, still, some part of that lovely and lordly man whom she had known so well, though for so short a time. No other of his family sur-vived, only that spark that was now beginning to kick and struggle as if to come untimely into the world.

Allitra sighed, looking downward. In the alien flatness of these plains, she also found comfort in the height of her dwelling. When her father had sent her from their mountain home, down to a wedding with a stranger in the flatlands, she had found her most wrenching moment when the last of the familiar peaks sank from her sight. The ridge of peaks that was visible from many spots in the Plains was hidden from Venelantir, so even that small thing was denied her.

And now, willy or nilly, she ruled here where the Ven had ruled for many lives of men. Yet, though her counse-

lors chided her for foolish fancies, she knew that somewhere in the hierarchy of Venelantir she had a bitter
enemy. They spoke of her pregnancy and the whims
women were wont to display when in that state. She had
pretended to believe, for she was uncertain of them all,
men and women, servants and soldiers alike.

Someone, she knew, had killed Kereno. She had
waked, the night he died, uneasy and disturbed. Rising,
she had gone down the short corridor to the room he used
for a study. There had been no lamp alight there, but
both moons had been in the sky, Ralias nearly at the full,
and the wide-windowed chamber had been filled with
cool light.

She could see Kereno, in silhouette, lying on the couch,
his hands raised before his face, his breath seeming to be
torn from his chest in great gasps. Before she could move
to his side or call for help, there had come one final gasp
. . . and a shape had risen from over his face and breast.
A shape of glimmer and shadow. A shape that had dwindled to nothing before her anguished eyes.

She had said nothing. Though young, she was intelligent, and her education had fitted her for rule. She well
knew that many had resented Kereno's choice of a wife of
Herreti blood and that they would seize on any excuse to
find her unfit to reign. Once lost to her, she knew that the
rule would not likely return to her child, however firmly
the law might affirm its claim. So she bided her time,
watching the suave statesmen come and go with scrolls
that must have her signature to become law.

In no great length of time, they had found that she
read what she signed, and she understood the design that
Kereno had had for his land. Nothing that would defraud
the people or the treasuries would she set her hand to. So
they hated her, but they respected her, too. Yet she greatly

suspected that whatever agency had seen to Kereno's death would attempt her own. There was a pattern to the fraudulent scrolls that she had refused to sign. There was a design to the coalitions and realignments that she could observe among those with whom she must deal.

Yet the designer was not to be found. Every great name, every wielder of power in the city came before her regularly, but in none of them could she find the deviousness, the ability, the focused wickedness that she felt to be at work about her. Soon she decided that there must be one who was not of the councils, not of the ostensible makers of law, who sat somewhere in shadow, wielding invisible strings.

She was cautious in her inquiries. Was there one, she would ask a wizened elder, who might be found to advise her—one not involved in the issues, who would be an objective voice?

That elder would look at her with fogged and concealing eyes and stammer, "Oh, no. No one at all." And she would know the lie.

It was a bit of servants' gossip that set her on the track, at last.

"They'm be out, last night." It was a girl's voice, soft and fearful. "Jannem be gone, this morn. Others, too, but Jannem my mum."

An older woman's voice crooned comfort, but the girl wept quietly.

"Why'm they not be stopped? Used, the Lord'd seal up the runs an' stop 'em in. Used, only once in a long time 'd they drag some'n under. Now there be no safe time."

The older voice said, bitterly, "They'll do 'un now. They'm be taken the great 'uns, too, not just us low. Cassira walken in the moons, last night. She'm not here, ever again. When the great 'uns start to go, they'm be sealed up again."

Allitra peeped through the curtains into the alcove where the two were folding linen. She recognized the girl as one who tended to her own mending.

She had raised her hand to brush aside the curtains when the woman whispered, "*He's* come up again. Once the Lord uz gone from us, he felt safe. He be old and old, true, but he be wicked more than all. Say nothing, see nothing. Keep in, nights, 'n lock you'm door. *He* be about again."

Allitra drew back her hand and turned aside into her bedchamber, as the two emerged, their arms piled high with towels. She resolved to take, at last, a maidservant to wait upon herself, though she had refused one, before. Her increasing awkwardness would make a fair excuse, she felt.

She waited several days. While it was unlikely that any save the two who spoke and she who listened had any notion of the conversation, she was cautious. Then she asked the girl, who was mending a (deliberately) torn robe, "What is your name, child?"

"Growem, Ma'am."

"I find, Growem, that I'm getting so tired and awkward I need one who will fasten my gowns and pick up the things I drop. Would it suit you to become my maid?"

The girl's blue-circled eyes rose for an instant to meet her own, then dropped again. But her voice showed her pleasure, though she said only, "I'd know honor, Ma'am."

So Allitra gave the orders, and none thought it strange. Indeed, all had thought it very strange that she had not wanted a personal servant before now, though it was recognized that her hardy mountain life had made her more independent than the slothful ladies of the city.

And Growem had proven to be a comfort that she had not foreseen. The girl was gentle, yet tough-minded. Her hands were strong and quiet, and her mind seemed untaught yet shrewd and logical. Long before Allitra had dared to begin trying for information from her, she had become a friend, the first that Allitra had found since losing Kereno.

So it was that the Lady of Ven found it easier than she had hoped to ask her handmaiden, "Growem, it has come to my ear that some peril visits my folk by night. No one will be clear as to its nature, and I am concerned. Also, I am certain that some person of great power is working his will in Venelantir, for I can see the signs of his movements. Can you tell me anything of these matters?"

She had chosen her time well. They walked in the garden of the palace, at the verge of an ornamental lake filled with scarlet fishes. The width of the lake and the gardens lay between them and the nearest part of the building. No shrubbery grew nearby to conceal an unwanted set of ears.

Perhaps for those reasons, perhaps because the young ruler had tried, very unobtrusively, to comfort the girl's unhappy heart, Growem answered her as fully as she could.

"Lady, there be dangers. Old ones, from days long gone, true, but new-risen to plague us. My own mum they took under, a time back, and I'll never see her more. There be . . . those . . . that live under, you see. Not on the lands we know, but under them. Always they'm be of dark evil. Always the Lord hunten 'um down and sealen 'um up, when they'm come up among us. For they taken folk down there into their black places, and none ha' ever come up again."

Allitra frowned. This had no sound of superstition but

of fact. In her own mountainous land, there was, or had been, a race that chose the caverns instead of the chill realms of light. And if Kereno had hunted these and driven them back into their burrows, then they must, indeed, be wicked beings. Her lord had held, in his wide-ranging mind, space for every sort of harmless creature and strange idea.

"And what of this one of power? Is there any knowledge of such? It is in my mind that my lord's death was not a natural thing."

Growem's eyes rose to meet hers. Behind them, her mind was working frantically, balancing newfound affection and trust with native caution. Then the girl said, "Ma'am, I lay my life in your hand."

The broad accent was gone, and her pronunciation was as clear as Kereno's own, as she continued, "I must tell you the truth, from past to present, if you are to know and understand what it is that you sense and fear. Jannem, my mother, was Kereno's 'mother-wife.' Among us it is custom for a young ruler to be entrusted to a good woman of some breeding when he reaches puberty. She teaches him the things he must know as a man and a husband. She is a comfort to him in those years when he lacks confidence. Too, she keeps him from the hands of those who would indulge his passions for their own profit.

"So it was with my mother and the Lord Kereno. And I am his child, whom he knew and loved, though he kept my existence a secret. It would have been a peril to me, you see. There are those who, even now, might find my existence to be . . . a lever."

Allitra nodded, comprehending. "So even your speech must conceal your origin."

"Yes. But now I am in great fear, for *He* has Jannem in His hands, if she still lives. And who knows what He might learn from her, if He should be moved to question her? She is strong, braver than most, but in the Underlands what would that avail her?"

"And who is He?" asked Allitra, very softly. "Who is this He who only dares to show himself when the Lord of Ven is in his grave?"

"The Sorcerer." Growem's voice was almost a whisper. "There have been those of his family active in the affairs of Venelantir since the times before legend. They are strong, they are clever, and they are, more than all, wicked. The first Ven was he who sent them under, harrying them from the upper lands. All since that first have kept a close eye upon their routes to the surface, making certain that they were sealed. How those below live, find air to breathe and water to drink, I dare not think.

"And now Salla tells me that He has been seen, himself, aboveground. It may well be that Lord Kereno came to his death by that hand. The Sorcerer has terrible crafts at his command, though he cannot exercise them, so it is said, through the barrier of earth. He must come up in order to weave his spells and to use his terrible contrivances against us who live in the light."

They walked in silence, slowly, along the verge of the lake, but their eyes did not see the artfully arranged lilies and rushes or the darting fishes. Each saw her own vision, and after a time Allitra turned her head to look full into the eyes of Growem.

"On the night my lord died, I woke in fear and went to see to him. He had worked late, and, as he was wont to do to avoid waking me, he had laid himself down upon his couch there. By the light of the two moons I could see his shape, see his hands desperately trying to thrust away some weight or obstruction upon his face and upper body. I heard his last gasp of breath. Then I saw a shape—like smoke or shadow, yet with a glimmer in it—rise up from him and dissipate into the air. I went back to my chamber, called for the guard, and said that I had dreamed ill, sending him to call my lord. I feared to say what I had seen, for they would delight to call me mad and thus steal the heritage from Kereno's child."

The younger woman drew in her breath sharply. "There have been more than one to die, of late, who showed no wound or illness. Do you remember Elzias, who commanded Kereno's guard? He went so, six nights ago. One of the Council of Elders, Garno of the Troadim, went so, two nights past. He was one of your few supporters in the Council, Lady."

"True," Allitra mused, looking away across the lake toward the Palace, where an ostentatiously busy gardener plied his trowel. "Find, if you can, how many among Kereno's true friends have died so, Growem. Can you do this without arousing suspicion?"

"I have only to open my ears, Lady. Such things are the talk of the lower levels in the Palace. The place is abuzz with the disappearances and the strange deaths."

"Good. This second thing I must ask as a great favor, and it may be so beset with danger that you will wish to say no. If that be true, then do not hesitate. I would do it myself, if I were not the custodian of Kereno's child."

"Ask, Ma'am. Then I will say."

"I must have access to my lord's workrooms, where he designed the weapons and the devices that were his passion. The chamberlain says that the keys have been impounded by the Council, until such time as one may be found to catalogue the contents and label the things as to danger. Yet I know that there were other keys than those my lord used. And someone has them, or their duplicates, for there has been light in those windows, shining through slits in the draperies, many nights over the past weeks.

"Can you look, as you go about the Palace, in every place possible, even the rooms of the chamberlain and the master of the guards? It will not be an easy thing to do, or a safe one. You may not succeed. But I know that there are keys somewhere, for Kereno said to me, once, that he had a hidden set, for use in the event of unforeseen betrayal. If he had only told me where they were!"

Growem's eyes grew bright. "This I will do, Lady, for you and for my father. I, too, have seen slips of light in windows where no light should be. And I know that you have need of every weapon that you can find. I often help Salla, when you have no need of me, and it will be no difficult thing to change linens or to polish their gewgaws. If there be keys to be found, be sure that I will find them."

Time moved heavily, now, for Allitra. Each day found her shorter of breath, wearier, and more downcast. And as Growem worked her way cautiously through the apartments of the Palace, without result, the Lady of Ven found herself growing apprehensive. Something, she felt with terrible certainty, was seeking for her through the nights; sleep became fitful, then nonexistent.

She fought her own fears for a week. Then she said to Growem, "Will you consent to sleep in my dressing closet? Twice I have dozed, only to wake with my breath stopped in my throat. It may be that only my fancy causes this, but for the sake of the child I must take no risk."

Since the loss of her mother, Growem had been a lonely woman, and her consent was not reluctant. So the nights found her within call, and the fact comforted Allitra.

As the days wore on, and the time came nearer for the birth of the child, she took thought to that, also. With Growem's help, she found trustworthy women to attend her, knowing that their presence would force the attendant midwife to ply her trade honestly. She would have named her own midwife, but that function was hereditary in Venelantir, one family having delivered every Ven for generations.

She also secretly drafted documents that she had Growem take into her keeping. Should she die, she was determined that Growem and none other should be the child's nurse and attendant. As guardian she named Carwen, the Lady of Ereon, who had been, she knew, Kereno's true friend, though now she held herself aloof from the affairs of Venelantir. She, Allitra felt, should be safe from the strange death, on that account.

Then, having done all that she could contrive to secure the well-being of the child to come, she composed herself as well as she could and waited. This was less easy, as the days of summer went forward. Her days were spent in walking slowly about the gardens, or in sessions with the Council, whose pleas for her approval now seemed endless as their supply of lettered parchment.

The effort of keeping her mind sharp and clear was the only refreshment in her uncomfortable days, and she almost welcomed the stream of importunate graybeards. Seated in Kereno's chair in Kereno's study, she judged each forthcoming petition as much by the look of its presenter as by the content of the crabbed writing. One who approached her wearing an expression of obtrusive frankness and honesty found his work examined with terrible thoroughness.

It was well. One day, near the end of her period of waiting, she found before her eyes a document that could have been made, with very minor touchings-up, to seem to be her will. Her signature would have validated it beyond question, if she were not alive to contest it. The disguised but unmistakable wording would have left Venelantir and the child of the Ven in the hands of "whatever worthy and wise guardian the Council might determine to be best."

She looked up and surprised the Councilman who had brought the thing to her. He had been staring intently at her, as if by force of will he might make her sign. She caught his eyes with her own, and though she said nothing, she saw guilt swimming there more visibly than her scarlet fishes swam in the Palace lake.

She laid the parchment by and set fingertip to fingertip. Her Councilman moved uneasily in his chair, and his face flushed faintly. She smiled.

"Grenon," she purred, "this seems a most presumptuous document indeed. I am well aware that women die in childbirth, and I have taken steps. My will is made, and it is in safe hands. Should the sad necessity arise, it will be delivered to the Council and to the people of Ven, simultaneously. Do not think, you of the Council, to take upon yourselves the responsibilities that are rightfully mine."

Grenon squirmed. "We only wished to help you, Lady. It is not a happy thought, the making of your own will. It was only an attempt at helpfulness. He . . . we are all concerned about your health and safety."

"I know quite well what it was," she sighed, motioning him away. "And this will remain with me, to be destroyed beyond reconstruction. You may tell Him that."

Grenon jumped, very slightly but visibly. His mouth opened, but she gestured again, this time so imperatively

that the guard beside the door moved forward to escort
him from the chamber.

When the two were beyond the door she looked again at
the document. It told her something that was not written
in letters of ink. They did not intend to allow her to live
beyond the birth of the child, if, indeed, until then. Her
fists tapped softly upon the shining wood of the tabletop.
How frustrating it was, after her strong and light-footed
life, to find herself thus imperiled at the very moment that
her body was only an impediment.

She could only take precautions, now, for it was beyond her to go seeking out her enemy. For now. Let the
child but be born safely, her strength return, and it would
be a different tale, indeed. Yet she had a friend and ally,
and she tapped the bell that brought Growem.

"It may be best," she said, in the softest of whispers,
"that the food sent to me only seems to be consumed. Can
you smuggle something to me from the kitchens that you
have prepared with your own hands?"

Growem's eyes narrowed. "So it has come to that," she
breathed. "It can be done, though I must avoid rousing
questions in the minds of the cooks and serving people."

"The precaution may be unnecessary. Indeed, I am almost certain that those whose purposes walk secretly in
Venelantir would scorn such forthright methods. Yet we
must take no chances, Growem. That is one. The finding
of a weapon perilous enough to frighten even Him is another. We must find the keys!"

Growem nodded, then she pretended to dust the alcove
behind Allitra's table, as she whispered, "I have taken a
step, Ma'am. It occurred to me that my closeness to you
might make me suspect. So I have placed Carwen
Ereonim's instructions in her hands, that my own death

might not leave my half-sibling friendless. I had the opportunity, and there was no time for asking you."

"A wise move. One I would have suggested, had I thought the chance might arise without being contrived. It comforts me to know that Carwen is warned. She is a bold lady, when it suits her to be."

Growem took down the light draperies and piled them over her arm, just as a firm rap sounded at the door. She curtsied deeply to the tall old hawk who entered, then slipped behind him out the door.

The newcomer bent his proud head only slightly to the Lady of Ven. Without being asked, he folded his thin, black-clad body precisely into the chair set for visitors. Though he looked her boldly in the eyes, Allitra noticed that his fingers twitched against his thigh, betraying his nervousness.

"It is unwise, Lady, for those unversed in the Law to draw their own documents," he said in a pedantic voice. "It leads to confusion, lack of clarity as to intent, many undesirable things. Though we devoutly hope that all goes well with you in the next days, still the succession must be protected, for the well-being of our country."

Allitra looked at him, knowing the full weight of his enmity. Then she took, deliberately, a bold step.

"Ashol," she said sternly, "I know exactly how your wishes lie. When I was brought as a bride to Venelantir you were full of welcome, until you found that I was made of stuff as firm as my mountains, not to be played upon in order to manipulate my lord. I have seen the trending of the documents you bring to me. Your wish now, as it has been, I suspect, for years, is to skim the wealth of Venelantir's treasuries into your own pouch.

"Kereno understood you. Only the influence of your family kept him from banishing you years ago, and so he told me from his own mouth. I will not sign anything that will allow you or one of your dupes to misapply funds. I will not empower you to control the military. I will keep you on as short a leash as can be managed. And when my child is safely born, I will bend all my might to keeping any part of his upbringing from being besmirched by you. Be warned. Warn your henchmen. Warn Him, if you dare approach Him."

She sat back to study the effect of her broadside.

Ashol turned gray. "You have no conception of the powers with which you are playing," he hissed, rising from the chair. "He is not to be warned, He is to be feared. You have put yourself into more danger than you know."

"More than Kereno found?" she asked, and he turned jerkily and left the room.

She sat for a time, after he was gone, considering. If she had succeeded in forcing the hand of Him, whoever He was, it would be well. Should He wait until she was weak and weary, during or after labor, she would be no match for the strange sendings that He could arrange. But if He would only try soon, before the birthing, she would be ready to battle Him. Kereno had been unwarned; she was not.

So it was that when Growem came that evening, with a small tray of bread and meat concealed beneath the newly washed draperies, she found her mistress busy in her sleeping chamber.

Allitra had placed lamps in odd nooks of the room, ready for lighting when the daylight failed. In the window she had hung a large prism shaped like an egg, from which dangled many silken threads that had been firmly tied to the loop from which the crystal hung.

In her bed was an artfully arranged bolster with the

light coverings draped so as to suggest a sleeping—and pregnant—form. Drawn back into the shadow of a corner was a deep armchair, and beside it was a table which held another prism, a glass of clear liquid, a ball of silvery thread, and a small, sharp knife.

Allitra chuckled as her handmaiden looked about her in bewilderment. "We of the mountains have our own ways of dealing with witchery and its like," she said. "In the deep places are to be found crystals with strange properties, if they be used by those who have the knowledge and the inborn gifts to operate them. I am no defenseless innocent, when faced with such things as killed Kereno. My need for a stronger weapon is for the time when I go hunting Him."

The girl gasped. "No one dares to hunt Him," she breathed. "Only the Lord Kereno would move to close Him away below the ground."

"Let me but bear my child and send him from harm's way, and I will hunt Him, indeed," Allitra said grimly. "Tonight I must hunt the thing He sends to slay me, for I hope that my boldness with Ashol has stung His pride, to the detriment of His wisdom. Will you help me?"

Growem looked about her. She shuddered, then drew herself straight. "I am my mother's daughter, as well as my father's. He has stolen her away from me, and He has killed my father, too. We are no weakling folk, we of the Emme. I will help you for them, for the child, for you . . . and for myself."

The light died. The moon Ralias was dark, and To-Sen, the other, was rising, giving little light as yet. The lights of Venelantir were kindled below, and for a time Allitra stood on her soaring balcony and looked out over the magical spectacle that was the city on a summer night. Then she went into her chamber and lit one lamp.

By its light, she began to work with the threads that hung from the window prism, attaching those on the left to the sides of the frame, those above and below to cornice and sill, and leaving those to right free, as yet.

Growem stood and watched, without comprehending, and Allitra took her hand, at last, and said, "When I call to you, go immediately to the window and fasten these remaining threads tightly to the frame on the right. I hope, this night, to trap the slayer of Kereno."

To-Sen moved slowly up the sky, and the lights of Venelantir began to go out. When the crescent moon twinkled in the waters of the lake, the last of the windows below were dark, and only the globed torches in the streets glimmered, still.

Allitra sighed and pushed aside her tray. "It will be time, soon, and I must quench my own lamp. But there are lightstones beside each, and after you fasten the threads, your next move must be to light every lamp. No matter what you see or hear, no matter what I seem to be doing . . . or suffering . . . the lamps must be lit. When that is done, stand beside me. I will need your strength to bolster my own."

Growem nodded. Then she cupped her hand about the crystal globe and blew out their only light. In the darkness, Allitra touched her shoulder as she passed on her way to the armchair that she had set ready. The two of them sat, quietly as ghosts, as the moon reached zenith.

There came, at last, a faint shimmering at the window. Not even by an indrawn breath did the two watchers betray themselves, as the prism twinkled fitfully with the thing's passing. When it was well into the room, its light increased, and it whirled in the middle of the floor, taking shape. When it was done, it seemed a thin cloud of vapor with tiny lightnings within.

Soundlessly, it swept to the bedside and flattened itself over the shape that lay there. When it was completely spread there, Allitra said, "Now!" and Growem darted to the window and secured the threads.

There was the scritch of the lightstone as Allitra spun the metal wheel against it, and the lamp beside her chair glowed. It was backed by a silver mirror that doubled its brightness. As Growem kindled the others, she found that they, too, were mirror-backed, so that the room swam in piercing brilliance.

The thing on the bed was no longer visible until Allitra rose heavily from her chair and took the second prism in her hand. When she held it before the lamp and spattered its light across the intruder, answering lightnings showed its location.

The thing began to slide from the couch, whirling upright again. Allitra reached down and lifted the goblet of water.

"Shiallis in haram oret!" she chanted, casting the liquid onto the shape in her chamber. The thing glowed green, plainly visible, now. The Lady took up the silvery thread and began to wind it about the quivering form, and where the thread touched, it clung.

The slayer now resembled nothing ever seen by man. Sapped by the light, it struggled feebly in its bonds, as Allitra stepped back from it. When she was beyond arm's reach, the thing whirled toward the window, but the pattern of prism and threads stopped it, and it spun mournfully in one spot.

"You, slayer of the Lord Kereno, tool of Him, are now banished from this world, which is none of your concern. I banish you with light! I banish you with water! I banish you with metal!" And she plunged the small knife into the center of the mass of greenish light and silver thread.

The thing winked out like a blown candle.

Growem moved to Allitra's side and lowered the exhausted woman to the bed. "Rest, now," she said, removing slippers and lifting away the bolster. "I will put out the lights and sit by you until morning."

"You have had no sleep," protested Allitra. "You need rest."

"You may require my attendance all day tomorrow," said Growem. "Who will know if I sleep or wake, here in your private chambers? Sleep, now, and I will watch. But I am sure that nothing will disturb us again, this night."

Allitra rose the following morning to a world beaten mercilessly by rain. The long span of drought and heat had found release, at last, in a storm of impressive proportions, and she wondered, eating her smuggled meal, if her success of the night before might have something to do with the changed weather. Well she knew that warlocks and sorcerers used the elements as weapons, when it suited their needs.

While Growem slept, the Lady sat in Kereno's study, interviewing the various supplicants who came with affairs of the City. Ashol was not among them. Neither, she noted with amusement, were any of the fraudulent documents that had cropped up almost every day since the Lord's death. She mentioned neither, however, and by midafternoon she was free of her duties.

The rain still poured, but she felt an access of energy that surprised her, after the past night's stresses. She wanted to be up and doing. She was relieved when Growem woke, for she had decided upon a bold plan.

Though Growem was taken aback by the scheme, she agreed at once to help her mistress in the project. The night that had just passed had revealed that the Lady of

Ven had strengths that none had suspected. So it was that the return of nightfall found the two tensely waiting.

It seemed long, indeed, before the Palace was quiet, its night lamps dimmed, and the myriad stirrings of the many tenants stilled. But that time came at last, and Allitra took a small bag of black cloth, flung a dark veil over herself and another over Growem, and led the girl from her chambers by a hidden door at the back of the dressing closet.

That let them into a dim corridor, which in turn led them to a service stairway going down from the highest point of the Palace to the lowest, with closed landings at every floor. When they reached the third landing, Allitra laid her ear to the panel and listened intently before laying her hand to the latch. The hall beyond the door was empty. Three doors were let into either side of it, and the two crept silently by them.

At the very end of the corridor was one single door, flanked by louvered vents. Like shadows, the women moved to it, and Allitra bent over the locking mechanism, while Growem listened for the footfall of any approaching guard. From the bag she carried, the Lady of Ven took a set of workmanlike lockpicks, a jar of light oil, and a feather, which she dipped into the oil and inserted into the lock. When it was well oiled, she set to work with her tools, working by touch, in the dim light.

There came, at last, a little click, and she lifted the heavy brass door handle and beckoned to Growem. The girl came in a rush, whispering, "There is a guard in the cross-corridor, making his round. We must secure the door, in case he might try the lock."

Allitra smiled and set the inner lock that also immobilized the handle. "He will have no clue that the door has been tampered with," she breathed. "We will be forced to work in the dark, lest the louvers betray a light, but To-Sen is well up. If we draw aside the draperies, that should give us a bit of illumination."

The work chamber was an orderly chaos of tables laden with strangely shaped devices, cabinets with shelves lined with tubing, fastenings, parts, and things less definable, with piles of parchment that evidently held the preliminary drawings for the things that Kereno intended to make. The little light of the moon was only enough to show them how much there was that must be seen clearly.

From her bag, Allitra took a small lightglass. "Draw the draperies again, Growem," she said softly. "We must have light. Perhaps we can find something with which to close off the louvering to the corridor." With a scritch, the lightglass kindled, and they rummaged about until they found large sheets of parchment, still uncut, that were thick enough to stop their little glimmer from betraying them.

Then they went to work in earnest. While Allitra went through the piles of plans, reading Kereno's small clear lettering that described the function of the device there depicted, Growem lit a candle and looked over the devices on the tables. The larger ones she ignored, but whenever she found one small enough to be carried in a pouch she brought it to Allitra and laid it on the drafting table at her side.

There came sharp clacks in the corridor, and both hurriedly quenched their lights, while the guard did his duty. They heard the door handle shift slightly to his touch, and they breathed twin sighs of relief when he moved away down the hallway.

"There will be another in a short while," Allitra said, turning more quickly through the plans. "We must find what we need and be gone, for light comes early, now, and the guards rise earlier still."

So they sped through their tasks, and when Allitra finally bent closely over one of the parchments, Growem had at her side every easily portable mechanism that she could find. When the Lady was done, she looked closely at the row of oddly contrived things beside her. She touched one, turned to read the plan, then set her hand upon another, similar yet smaller.

"This, if anything, is what we seek. Take down the parchment, Growem, while I straighten the plans. We must be gone from here quickly."

They listened when they went into the corridor, for the sound of heels upon stone, but all was silence. Then Allitra locked the door. Growem lifted the thing they had found, and the two sped to the service stair again. Before they had reached it, there came a sound down the cross-corridor, then a mixture of sounds.

"Orders said to break into the Lord's workroom," boomed a voice in the stillness. "Someone saw a light in the window. Hurry on, there, Kalek. Immediately, the Watchmaster said."

The two veiled figures whisked into the landing, and the door slid shut behind them, just as the clatter of boots emerged into the main hallway. "Thanks be to all the gods that we put things aright again," murmured Allitra. "Yet who could have known that we were there? Unless He . . ."

"If you have seen light there, then it is He who has been there," said Growem. "It well may be that He has no idea of the purposes and uses of my father's inventions and has been simply studying them. He has no need, as we have, of a weapon. At least, He has no present need of such, though I am certain that He will use all, if given

the chance, against us and all those who refuse to give
Him homage."

"If the thing I have chosen is the thing that Kereno described to me, then it will ensure that He will have no opportunity to harry my people," Allitra answered.

The hallway into which they emerged was still empty,
but there was a stirring behind the closed doors as they
hurried along it to the spot where the hidden mechanism
opened the secret door into Allitra's chambers. It was with
much relief that Allitra heard the panel slide into place
behind her.

She was breathing hard, and a stitch in her side was
making itself felt, as she sank upon her couch. Growem
touched her hand, concerned, but she managed a smile.

Dawnlight was creeping into the room as she stretched
herself to sleep, but even as she dozed away she heard a
muted disturbance, deep in the Palace, and knew that her
night's endeavor had set her enemies astir. Then she felt a
change within herself. There was no pain, no actual
movement of the child, but as if a voice had spoken into
her ear she knew that the coming day would see the birth
of Kereno's child.

"Call the midwives, Growem. Tell them that before
nightfall I will need them. Now I must sleep, if I can, but
the child is ready," she said. In the next breath, she was
asleep.

Growem drew the blinds against the growing light.
Then she went to the study and looked from the doorway,
summoning the sleepy guard who had stood there all the
night.

"Send word to the Councillors," she said. "There will
be no audience today, for the Lady of Ven is preparing for
the birth of the Heir. Send Salla to me, also. There is
much to do, this day."

Salla soon came, for she rose early to attend her multitudinous tasks. Growem sent her after the women she had chosen to attend the birth, though she contented herself with sending a formal request, by way of the guard, to the Midwife of Ven. Then she settled herself on her own couch to rest, knowing that the time might well be short.

She woke to find Allitra standing beside her. "It is past midday," said the Lady. "It might be well to call those who will have me in care, for the time is drawing near."

Growem rose at once, much refreshed, and saw that the windows held, each one, a prism. They were of different shapes, varying colors, and some were many faceted, while others held only a few finely cut planes through which the light angled oddly.

"Let them draw no draperies," Allitra said, pacing to and fro and breathing carefully. "Say that it is my order. Watch, Child, oh watch the Midwife of Ven. I am uncertain of her . . . more than uncertain. I am sure in my inmost mind that He has tampered with her. Warn the others to take the child immediately into their own hands, as soon as he is born. I want her to have no chance to do him ill." She paused and clenched her hands together for a long, slow breath. Then she nodded.

Growem went into the outer chamber that was joined to the study by a short corridor. There she found the women waiting, and she spoke to them very quietly, warning them as she had been instructed. Then she went to the study, where the Midwife waited, sitting apart from her lesser assistants. With her were the members of the Council, who immediately set up a babble of questions and suggestions.

Ashol quieted them with a gesture and said to Growem, "It is the custom, as well as a sensible precaution, for one or more members of the Council to attend the birth of an Heir. One of us must go with the Midwife."

Growem looked into his eyes, thinking with furious clarity. "You will do as well as any," she said. "But you must wait in the dressing closet. There you will be in no one's way, yet you may see and hear everything." She was relieved to see him turn pale. He had, she knew, expected resistance to the notion, yet she felt that it was best to have that slippery Councillor under her eye at this crucial time.

The three went back down the way, finding that the women had preceded them into the inner chamber. Already they were busy, setting up the birth-chair, showing the Lady how to control her breathing, swathing every surface in clean linen, and laying out the toweling and the oil for the infant's first bath. As the Midwife entered all bent their heads in respect, but they paid no attention at all to Ashol.

Ashol, however, set one foot within the room and stopped. The light from the prism in the western window struck through the chamber with pitiless brilliance, casting volleys of rainbows onto the walls and the ceiling. The tall man seemed to wince as the brightness touched him, and it seemed, for a moment, that he might withdraw entirely. Yet he only wavered for a moment. Then he followed Growem's gesture and scuttled into the dressing closet like some dark rodent to its burrow.

It was a long birthing, though not a terribly hard one. The Lady made no sound more than groans of effort as the birth came to completion. The child emerged into the hands of the Midwife, who took an instant to glance triumphantly toward the closet where Ashol sat. In that span, one of the women lifted the whimpering baby from her grasp and bore him away to the others. Then it was too late, for the Midwife must now busy herself with tending Allitra, her opportunity lost.

Growem, watching all, hearing all, did not miss the faint curse from the unseen Ashol. She smiled internally, as she stepped forward to take the child, now cleaned and clothed, for his first formal meeting with his mother.

Allitra took him in exhausted arms and held him closely. "All will bear witness who attended this birth: This is the true son born to the Lady of Ven and to Kereno, her departed lord. I have prepared a scroll upon which you may, if you will, set your seals and signatures, as you leave. And for your refreshment, Growem has prepared a supper for you, together with gifts of gratitude from me."

They set things to rights, then, offering to tend the Lady also, but she waved them aside. "I am so weary that I must rest, even before bathing away the sweat of my labors. Growem, who knows my ways, will help me in a bit. Go now to your reward, with my affection and thanks."

They stood back until Ashol, his face a study in stiffness, kissed her hand and moved away. Then each did the same, and Growem followed them into the outer chamber, where the scroll lay waiting. The women waited for Ashol to sign first, as was fitting, but he seemed to have difficulty with the matter. The quill and the ink seemed not to his liking. Then his hand was unsteady and blotted his first attempt. Yet he could not refuse. These were no servants but ladies from good and respectable families in Venelantir. They could not be ordered to silence, compelled to obedience, or made to lie. He was caught in the trap that Allitra had made, with Growem's help.

As it was, the ladies went to their repast with many

questions in their minds as to the motives of Ashol, Councillor of Venelantir. There could have been no legitimate reason for his hesitance to sign the scroll, save only one, and that they knew to be false. That night there was rejoicing in the city, but there were also questions asked among the solid merchants and professional men, whose wives had attended the Lady.

So it came about that the city was alert, and the strange workings that had riddled the summer labors of the Council subsided in the light of suspicion.

The babe was strong and well-made. He had the look of her own mountain family, though he owned Kereno's eyes and stubborn chin. He was alert, too. Growem swore that she had never seen an infant so young follow folk with his eyes as they spoke.

Allitra's joy in him was tinged with pain. He brought back to her the loss of his father, true, but there was a deeper reason. She knew that even as he slept and ate and grew, the enemy of his family was plotting against him. Only she stood between her child and death . . . or subjugation to an evil will.

So she tended the child with love and tears, and on his naming day she stood in the great audience chamber of the Palace and called out his name to the gods, "Karas, Ven of Lantir, ruler of the City in the Plain, son to Kereno of the Ven and Allitra of the Herreti."

A great shout went up, for the people of the city had known great security and prosperity under the rule of the Ven. The shadows that now seemed to gather about their land had come since the loss of their lord, and they felt that the accession of a Ven, even an infant one, would make all right again.

Then there was a time of quiet. Allitra worked at growing strong again, exercising in her chamber until she was irritated by the confinement, then running and climbing and lifting weights in the guards' training rooms, using them at night when none were about. Growem watched with growing concern, feeling the existence of some dangerous purpose, but Allitra told her little.

Allitra sent for Carwen, some weeks after the birth. Her ostensible reason was to show her husband's oldest friend his son, but while the lady was with her she told her 'many things and commended both Karas and Growem to her care. Carwen listened quietly, said little, but when she went away Allitra was comforted. Whatever happened, her son would be protected, she felt certain.

Yet she felt the approach of some catastrophe. It breathed through her sleep and in her dreams. It hummed at the edge of perception in the day. He, whoever He was, was at work, there beneath the Plain, and she felt the pulse of His power as it grew. All the talents of her wild mountain clan woke in her, and she studied the faceted crystals, tuning herself to them. Though they could not show her that mysterious One, they did make clear the distortions that He was making in the soil and the air of the city. Even the river gave strange emanations, and she shuddered to think what terrible weapon He might have devised, wedding his wicked mind to Kereno's stolen arts.

There came a day when she called Growem to her. "Take the child and goodly supplies of his necessities," she said. "Call Salla and what other of the people of the Palace you judge to be true. Send them to their homes to get their folk and their goods together. Then come with me to Carwen. I am declaring a grand holiday for all Venelantir. All must go to the mountains to give thanks for the safe delivery of the Heir. Such is the custom of the Herreti, and it is fitting that it be followed."

There was much resistance to her decree. Still, Carwen and a few of her intimates stood by the Lady, and with much grumbling the people of Venelantir found themselves on an unwanted holiday, moving toward the mountains. Many of the Councillors refused to go, together with most of the guard and a number of the more suspicious tradesmen who would not leave their goods, come what may.

Growem thought her Lady to be traveling with Carwen. Carwen believed her to be with her own train from the Palace. By the time they realized that she was not among them at all, it was too late to go back and search for her. But they said nothing, for each suspected that some terrible danger hung over the city that Allitra intended to circumvent.

And it was true. With much relief, Allitra saw the dust trails thin out upon the Plain as her people and her son departed. Now she could battle Him in any way that she could find, without endangering her own.

She stood at her window, watching, until the last sign of travelers disappeared. Then she turned, with one last glimpse of the joyful whirls that marked the balconies, and took up a pack that lay ready on the table in her bedchamber. She listened. No sound rose from the city, though the sun was not yet down. The Palace was quiet, for even those who had refused to leave the city had been sent to their homes. No one guarded the structure. No cook or serving man or maid moved within it. There was none to observe her presence or her going.

Still, she went cautiously, through the secret doorway, into the network of service corridors and stairways. This time she went down to the very bottom of the stairwell. At its end there were three doors, all closed. She opened that on the left and stepped out into the earthy scent of the deepest cellar, where wines and root crops were stored.

It was dark past the thought of darkness. When she closed the door behind her, hiding the glimmer of the lamps in the stairwell, the blackness was fit to suffocate her. She felt blind panic rise in her throat and remembered her old hatred of enclosed spaces. But now there was no avoiding it. She must go far deeper than this.

From her pocket she fumbled one of the prisms and rubbed it between her hands. After a time, it began to glow.

The light was a strange topaz color, seeming to emanate as much from its surroundings as from the stone. It cast no shadow, yet it allowed her to see her way. That way was a thing of terror to her. Among Kereno's diaries she had found an account, years old, of a breakthrough from the lower ways into the Palace itself. It had been carefully sealed, yet she thought of the light in the workroom and knew that it had been unstopped. Probably before Kereno's death.

She made her way among the bins and wine racks, keeping account of every turn. At last she found herself faced by a wall that seemed to be made of solid dressed stone. Damp oozed down the oily surface, and she could see no trace of crack or join that might lead to her goal. Yet she knew without doubt that this was the place she sought.

She felt for another prism, laying the first on her pack, which she had set aside for the moment. The talents of her folk were strange, and the prisms served as a focus for their energies, though she had been told that only a belief in their necessity made them so. Still, the hard, angled shape in her hand reassured her, as she set her will against the stone, feeling, pushing, pulling at the obdurate surface.

Sweat sprang onto her eyelids, trickled down her nose. She felt her muscles tensing and deliberately eased them, breathing deeply as she did so. There! A hint of motion had followed her willing. She set herself against the rock, mind against matter, and felt the big block of stone quiver, grating in its place, then begin to move. It swung out too easily. It had been recently used, she felt sure, or it would have required much more effort on her part.

She set it ajar, just enough for her to slip by. Then she took up her pack, pocketed the second prism and held the first in hand, and entered, shuddering. A few strands of cobweb brushed her hair as she went through. That confirmed her belief. If twenty years had passed since this way had been used, there would have been masses of the things.

A chill draft moved in the way. By this she knew that the door into the Palace was only one point along a tunnel dug for other purposes entirely. She moved into the breeze, feeling in some intuitive way that that would lead her where she must go. The glow of her prism seemed overbright, so she wrapped it again and set it in her pocket. In this straight way, there was little likelihood of losing her way.

It seemed a long time, indeed, that she walked, feeling the stony rubble beneath her boots. Then her foot clicked on smooth stone, and she stopped instantly and listened. There was the drip of water, to her right. Ahead, in the blackness, she could hear movement. Slithery sounds like bare feet on paving stone. Other sounds, like whispers, yet somehow unlike.

She took a deep and silent breath. It was for this that she had come. The fate of Venelantir was in her hand, and to falter now would be to condemn her son and all his folk to a slavery that beggared all other sorts. Unconsciously, she straightened her back. Her head went up, and her eyes strained into the darkness.

When the hand touched her face she almost cried out, but she damped it to a gasp. A chittery voice gabbled beside her, but she could make out no words that she knew. Then other hands caught her, tore away her pack, fumbled through her pockets, discarding the prisms as mere stones, she thought. One of them remained in her pocket.

In the darkness she smiled, as she heard one of the creatures grunt under the weight of the pack. Let them take it where they would; so long as it remained underground, it would still serve her well.

A light began to grow about her, and she realized that she stood in a great hall. The tunnel that she had followed entered the place through an ornate doorway, and she could see that intricate mosaic lay beneath her feet. She looked closely about her, at the great globes that were blossoming to light, the walls that were painted with hideous accuracy, anything except her captors.

They had been human. They still were, possibly, but they were well on their way to beasthood. Pale as grubs, they had huge, blinking eyes, shaggy, colorless hair. They were hung about with cloths of varying shapes and hues, but those were evidently for ornamentation, not for clothing. All in all, they were a hideous crew, the more so because some were almost fully human and others were almost entirely beast, with all gradations between.

"You find my people beautiful?" asked a sardonic voice.

She turned her eyes toward it, without haste. She saw a blade-slender form clad in scarlet. The face, as the light grew brighter, became clear, and she looked long at her enemy for the first time.

"You are of the family Elosi," she said. "You are like enough to Ashol to be his brother."

The figure shook with silent laughter. "Say rather his father," he chuckled. "I got him on his mother, then turned her again into the light whence I had plucked her. It is often useful to have agents aboveground. None of the Elosi had brains enough to dream that that one might not be of the pure stock."

Allitra looked with loathing upon him, noting that he seemed not even of an age with his son. "So you are of no family belonging to Venelantir," she said.

"Venelantir is not the name of the land above," he growled, "and it is a bauble belonging to my family, not otherwise."

"Being presently cluttered with folk who would not honor your claim, no doubt," she said, her voice so quiet that he bent nearer to hear. "I have known your workings, both aboveground and below, Sorcerer. We of the Herreti are not without sorceries of our own. The . . . visitor . . . that you sent to my chamber found my welcome wanting in cooperation. He, it, whatever you call the thing, will not come again to your summoning."

Now the great clusters down the length of the hall had reached full brilliancy, and by the white light she could see angry color mount into his pale face. The creatures had retreated before the illumination, leaving her pack beside her, and she sat upon it and laughed.

"You are in my kingdom, now," He said furiously. "You will have no cause to laugh, ever again. I shall mate you to the least of my people. You will produce a stream of shaggy and mindless thralls for my uses. Evil for you was the time you fell into the hands of my scourers."

She laughed harder. "I came of my own will," she choked, between chuckles. "I moved the stone wall in the lowest cellar of the Palace. I followed my sensing down the black tunnel until my foot touched the paving of this hall. I found your beasts, not they me. I hunted you to your lair, Enemy, Slayer of Kereno, threatener of my son and his subjects. Now I have you in my grasp, and you cannot escape."

His pale eyes glittered. "Your wits are unsettled, woman! Even now, I feel the rock beneath us beginning to tremble in the convulsion that will shake down enough of your prized city to bring its inhabitants to their knees. This night will see Venelantir humbled, kneeling to its rightful lord!"

She stood, her bright head level with his own. She looked eye into eye, as she said, "I have sent all who would leave to the mountains to give thanks for the new Heir. Only a few of your lackeys still walk in the city. My son is far off, in good hands, and he will grow up in the northern mountains, safe and strong.

"I have come to slay you, and to die with you, for only so will I know your evil seed to be gone from the land."

She glanced at the pack, and it trembled. As the vibration in the bedrock below their feet grew, so did the shaking of the pack. An angry hum rose from it, and she set her will upon it, forcing it, through the great crystal within her pocket and the device inside the pack, upon the entire plate of rock that lay beneath Venelantir.

He threw up his head, unsettled. "Ashol's son, my grandson, is safe!" he cried. "I required him of his father, sent him to another place to be taught in my own way. You cannot be rid of us so easily!"

"Then let there be no city for him to rule!" she shouted, as the world seemed to tilt beneath her. She saw her enemy dart for the tunnel door, and she followed him, over the heaving mosaic, under the globes that now began to dim with the withdrawal of His attention.

The world gnashed its stony teeth all about, as she ran down the tunnel. Stones and soil were falling about her, and she took her prism in hand, that she might see to avoid new-fallen debris. She could see by its strange light glimpses of scarlet in the dust before her, and she knew that He still moved.

She caught Him as He worked at the passage through the wall. With all her strength, she held the stone fast shut, as He struggled to force it open. The prism grew hot in her hand, glowing like an ember of fire. The stone, caught between two opposing forces, quivered with more than the agony of the land about it. With a final shudder, it collapsed into rubble, and He shouted, as He leaped across it, into the cellar of the Palace.

With a grinding roar, the structure fell in upon itself, and Allitra saw a huge beam fall squarely atop the Sorcerer. Dust filled the passage, choking her, and she turned away, fumbling among fallen portions of the tunnel, hoping that its other end still led wherever it had been designed to go.

She stumbled out into a world of dust and darkness. The tunnel ended in the midst of a pile of artfully arranged stones at the edge of the river, and she rolled forth and fell on her knees, staring, aghast, at the place where the city had been.

A tremendous gash knifed through the arc where the river had flowed. Boiling floods growled and churned their way through the new passage, where no trace of any structure now remained. The spot on which she knelt now stood high on the edge of a cliff that fell sheer into the new channel. All the place where the city had stood had sunk on the west of the chasm and risen on the east. Any who came again to Venelantir would never know that he stood upon the spot where it had been. Under the light of two moons, as the dust blew away on the freshening wind, she saw what she and the Sorcerer, between them, had done.

She looked away into the north. There her son and all his people would be sheltered and safe with her own folk. But she, who had destroyed his birthright, deserved nothing of them.

She turned her face southward, toward the distant ocean that she had never seen, and began to walk.

Varil opened her eyes. So vividly had she lived the segment of time that it was some moments before she reoriented herself. Her fire had burned low, and she was stiff with effort, and with sitting.

Her dark eyes still saw the devastation that had been the City in the Plain. The dust still tickled her nostrils, and the night wind was cool about her ears.

She sat, watching the embers darken. Then, with an effort, she rose and replenished the blaze, set the kettle of soup nearer to boil, and went to the window.

A spat of snow drove against the glass, then more. As she listened, the wind began to moan in the forest that lay about her house, and she knew that upon the mountains and out in the Plain it would be bitterly cold.

Her supper eaten, she sat once again before the blaze, examining the store of new knowledge that she had found. The Sorcerer—yes! She understood more than she had, far more, of the new Lord of Lantirion. He could be defeated, even as his long-ago ancestor had been.

And Karas Lantir, co-tenant of her heart, must indeed

be the distant descendant of that valiant lady who had brought down the city and the Sorcerer together. Much that she had found in him was now explained, including that odd talent he had for moving pebbles without the use of his hands.

Yes, now there could be a plan. With the threads in her hands, stretching away into the past, out into the present, forward into the future, she could now begin to find her way through the maze of problems that beset her land.

She closed her eyes again and thought of Karas Lantir . . .

CHAPTER 1

The quall were hunting. I could hear their thin wails.

I lay flat, just under the lip of the ridge. The cold of the stone beneath crept up through the fur lining of my tunic and my belly muscles cramped with it—and with apprehension. Raising my head as carefully as a hunting cat, I felt the chill wind knifing by my ears as I peered over the rough outcropping that hid me from the plain beyond.

I curled down into a ball, nursing the pain in my ribcage. From my position, I could see the still collection of lumps that was my horse, and I cursed the Warlock, the quall, the catlike hunters of the high places that had killed my mount behind me, when I stole ahead on foot to spy out the land from the ridge. With darkness nearly here, the cold, and the splinter that the Warlock must even now be driving deeper into my image, it looked to be a long night.

The years of cold vigils and hard sleeping had made me tough, but they hadn't made me like it. I thought of Varil's hut, rude and comfortless-looking from the path in the wood surrounding it, but lined with furs and silken tapestries that I had brought back to her from many odd corners of the kingdom my father had lost to the Warlock on a roll of the dice. I sighed. Warm soup and hot bread from her fire would burn the chill from my bones, and the pain of the Warlock's diggings with his needle would ease with the warming. But here I was and I was not intending to die of it.

The last rays of the sun reached beneath the edge of cloud that lay over the next range of mountains. They picked out a familiar dark streak in the stone beside me, and I grinned. The Devil takes care of his own, they say. It's a bit puzzling, for I would have thought the Warlock was dear to his heart. Maybe some divinity had taken my fate in hand.

I took my knife from its sheath, ignoring the stabbing agony that moving caused, and began picking chunks of coal out of the rock. When I had a sizable pile, I crouched over it and took my tinder box from its pouch in my cloak. When the spark caught, at last, in the fuzz and kindled the coal, I stayed over it, burning the pain from my ribs. Then I went down to the horse and retrieved my saddle pack.

With food and fire, I was fairly well content, though the wails of the quall drew nearer. They would see the fire. They might just be hungry enough to stalk the man they associated with flames. But I had my sword to hand, its keen two-edged blade bared and ready to hand. And my dagger lay securely against my hip. I shaved with it, when the fit took me.

After eating, I lay back against the rock that the fire was warming and wrapped my cloak securely—but cunningly—around me. My right hand was covered, but free. My left, also, though no watcher would have believed it to be so. My eyes grew heavy, and I dozed, rousing now and again to feed the flame from my rock pile.

As I drifted in that no-world between waking and sleeping, I found Varil's face coming before my eyes. I opened them a slit, and the red-gold of the fire mingled with the red-gold of her knotted hair. The dark blots of coal became her black eyes. She nodded, surveying me as if she were there before me. "You'll do," she said. "Not too well, it seems, when you leave my protective influence, but well enough."

I grunted. "Enough of your sauciness, wench. Why do you make your witcheries with me?"

"Karas Lantir, my witcheries are made in your behalf, as you well know. I have news for you—but while I was making the effort to reach you, I looked about over the lands. You'll have company in a couple of hours."

"Quall?" I asked.

"A great pack of them. You're in a tight spot, friend Karas. I see you've lost your horse, too. And the Warlock, our new and well-beloved" (here her lip curled delicately) "ruler has widened his ban on you. Now you are not to be aided or answered. And a bounty has been laid upon your head, which he prefers to have detached from your body before the reward is claimed. Such outcry arose against your banning that he hanged a score or more of your subjects in order to silence it."

I growled. My father and I are not overtender of the hides of our subjects, but not one of them has ever laid his death to us in an unjust cause. My hands clenched, and the stab in my side made me gasp.

"Would that I could conjure away that invisible wound," said Valir, glimmering in the firelight. "That, however, none but the Warlock can do, unless someone finds a way into his chambers and steals away the image itself, gently to remove the splinter from its side."

"It is well enough," I said. "What of my father? Have you looked to his safety?"

"He lies hid in the mountains with his old huntsman. Illness has altered him. You'd be hard put to recognize the tough old bog-root you embraced when you parted a year ago. When he sobered, after gaming away the kingdom that was his—and your—heritage, his guilt wore inward on him, affecting his heart, I think. His chest pains him, and his breath is short, these days."

Her image glimmered, as a coal flared and broke. Her voice was thinner, distant, as she said, "Care for yourself, Karas. You are the hope of Lantirion. Take thought! Take thought to the Warlock!" And she was gone.

The fire was dying. Though I had intended keeping a blaze for the night, I changed my plan. Quall two hours away were infinitely too nearby for me. Men I had never feared, or hunting cats, or any other thing that lived on my lands. But the quall were small and verminous and hunted in packs that numbered thousands. Their wails hurt the ears and the mind, and when a man fell, he was eaten to the bone while one might count to ten.

I stirred the embers with my toe, knocking them apart. The snow that was beginning to fall in fitful gusts would extinguish it, though there was nothing on these barren heights to concern even a careful woodsman like me. When my cloak was fastened securely over my fur tunic, I hefted my saddle pack. Too heavy by half. So I winnowed out the food, the earthen bottle of water and wine, the fur leggings, which I donned immediately, blessing Varil who had insisted that I bring them. The rest I discarded, regretting the heavy blankets, but knowing that my cloak was sufficiently thick and warm to do duty for them.

I knew better than to leave my belongings lying about for quall—or man—to find. I climbed high up a rockface and stuffed them into a dark hole, filling in the opening with loose rubble from a ledge just below it. Then I bundled my burden in a woolen shawl and set off to traverse the ridge, just under the highest point.

I went northward, and the wind that cut madly out of

the northeast was partly deflected by the backbone of the mountain. The stony ledges and loose screes would take a poor trail, I well knew, but I knew also the tenacity of the quall. Before dawn, if my calculations were correct, they would catch up with me.

I found what I sought at last, a narrow cut that led through the ridge onto the sheer face of the cliff that rose here in unclimbable smoothness above the plain. The sides were sheer and went up hundreds of feet. My bulk all but filled the cleft. Nothing could come at me from behind—nothing that breathed and bled. A sharp angle ten paces into the cut broke the ferocity of the wind, so that I could make shift to sleep for a bit, with one eye open and both ears honed.

So I dozed, cold and aching beneath my ribs, while the beasts came up behind me. It was near dawn when I heard them wailing along my trail, and I roused myself and stretched my muscles, shrugging from them the worst of the night stiffness. I laid my dagger by my left hand and held my sword in my right. Then I waited.

And they came. The Devil—or whoever was taking a hand—granted that they came with first light, so none could creep by to seize me from below. They came with the rush that is their way and a fury that is not. Cruel and hungry they have always been, but the red ferocity of their attack made me wonder, as I slashed gray bodies and skewered them on the dagger and kicked them over the precipice beyond the trail, if some spell had not been laid upon them.

Then I had no time to wonder. They came. They came. Hundreds died, and my blades dripped and puddles of blood formed at my feet. A mound of mangy-furred bodies began to rise, though I kicked them clear as often as might be. Still came that thin wail from my back trail, as if there were no end to the swarms of things.

I wearied. Dawn gave way to sunrise, though no sun could be seen behind the snow clouds. The day wore to midday. I was gory from head to heel, bitten and gashed so that my own blood mingled freely with that of the quall. My arm, hardened though it was to long and deathful battles, swung more slowly. Quall began to break through the arc of my stroke, taking, each time, more of my flesh, letting free more of my blood.

At last my gaze began to waver, and I thought, *Is this the way the Heir of Lantirion must die, gnawed to rags by vermin on the backbone of the world?*

As if in answer to my despair there came a wind through the cleft at my back. It was so strong that I was swept from my feet, though my bulk is great and no such wind had I ever found before. I rolled against a boulder and hugged it as if it were Varil herself, while that furious gale swept the cleft and the path clear of quall. More came into the cut, and more were flung over the precipice beyond it. For what seemed hours, that cleaning went on, while I froze to the boulder, uncertain if it were much better to die of cold than to be eaten by quall.

Still, the remnants of my fur garments were left to me, and I took what comfort I could from them, though I could not loose my grip to rearrange them. And fewer quall came to be slain by the wind. The force of it died, by degrees, and no more beasts moved within my view.

I tried to loose my grip on the boulder, but it took effort to make my cramped muscles unclench. When I stood, at last, and was able to walk to the edge of the precipice that had swallowed so many of my enemies, I could see, far below, what seemed to be a mounded hill. I knew it to be

the fallen quall, and I thanked the gods, known and un-
known, for that fortuitous wind.

The pain under my ribs cannot be explained or imag-
ined. I stood erect, for I knew if I gave in to it I would
surely fall there and never stir again. Under its roweling,
I stumbled to the other end of the cut and looked out over
the lowlands that swept away in grassy undulations to the
distant foothills that marked the range of mountains on
our eastern border. There lay the stronghold of the Warlock, who did not deign to inhabit the paltry castle he
won from my father.

Something inside me urged me toward that distant
blur, though snow now fell between, making those mountainous shapes waver and disappear. I thought again of
Varil's parting words. And a sudden fury warmed me
from within. I had not cried out against my father's disas-
trous folly, though I had known that no common drink
could possibly have made my sire drunk to foolhardiness.
I had not accused the Warlock of the things I knew he
must have done. Honor dictated that I stand by my father
in this, as in all other things, and I had taken the small
count of things that were mine by purchase and gift and
had gone to Varil, fairly well content that I need not keep
my secret love hidden, any more.

By no word or sign had I raised any ire against the new
king. But a villain takes all men for villains, and he had
mistaken my quietude for hidden plotting. So the ban was
declared, which was a brutally unjust thing. And now I
was game for any brigand's steel.

I am not a patient man. Had I not been secretly glad to
be rid of the cares of a kingdom, the Warlock might well
have had cause to fear me. But enough was more than a
sockful, as my old nurse had said when I went that one
step farther than her patience would stretch. Now I was

warm, indeed, with anger. Now I must see that wily man, face to face, and charge him with his misdeeds, or honor would perish from my life and my world.

I seemed to feel Varil's warm hand on my cheek, just for an instant. Her voice, less than a whisper, moved in my ears, "Now, Karas, you find the path! You are more than any skulking wizard who ever drew breath. This one who dogs you is helpless without trickery and deceit. You, in and of yourself, have more potencies than even you know. You aided me in bringing that wind against the quall. You can move things with your will . . . think on that, and remember the many times you have done such things to amuse your father's drinking mates. Hold fast to yourself! Take care!" and then the voice was gone entirely.

Shrugging my tattered furs about myself, I kicked about among the stiffening quall until I found my pack. Then I turned back on my trail to the place where I had begun the night, for I knew that I must contrive better clothing than what was left to me now, if I were to survive the trek across that snow-ridden plain.

It took a bit longer to go than it had done to come. Without the impetus of pursuing quall . . . and with the hindrance of dozens of stiffening bites and cuts, the way seemed longer. But I reached the charred rock where my fire had blazed, at last, and looked upward, seeking for the hole where I had hidden my possessions. Once I had spotted it, it was another thing entirely to climb that sheer face to retrieve them. One foot was bitten, through the boot, almost to the bone, and its support was not trustworthy. My right hand was swollen and almost totally stiff from the hours and hours of sword-wielding. And the rest of me was a good match for my battered extremities, with the Warlock's gift still digging viciously under my ribs.

Still, I made it up, with much resting on invisible footholds and a heart-stopping number of near falls. I dropped the things gratefully to the stony cup below, and then I jumped atop them, for I knew that my outraged muscles would never see me safely down by way of unseen notches and clefts. But I didn't stop to rest. I wrapped myself in segments of the heavy fur blankets, binding the strips about me with torn-off lengths of my tattered cloak. When I was done, I buried what I could not carry beneath a tumble of stones.

Then I set off, as I had intended to do before the quall interrupted me, to descend the mountain ridge by way of the precarious trail that I had been following. It was no highway, be assured of that. Few, if any, knew of it who had not hunted with my father and me in these mountains. It was almost impossible for a horse to negotiate (though I had intended attempting it on mine, before the cats got him). For one burdened with packs and wounds, it was a hell of ice and loose stony patches and vertiginous passages above sheer drops of thousands of feet. I made the descent slowly, and part of the time I think I was hallucinating, for I had a long conversation with my father over what I must say to the Warlock when I found him.

CHAPTER 2

The plains, when I reached them, were worse. Snow had drifted against the slopes, driven by the howling wind that seemed to have no end and no beginning. The flatland was chest deep in most places, and the day was well done before I reached that stage of my journey.

I well knew that I must have heat, or I would die and be lost from the eyes of all save Varil. There was no growth of any kind standing above the snows, though I knew that winter-killed grasses abounded below it. But they were wet and inaccessible, so I thought of Varil's words that had whispered to me. And a way appeared.

There was no lack of stones—great boulders and shelves of rock had split, over the aeons, from the heights above and rolled their ways into the lands below. I picked a chunk the size of a barn, one with an overhang like a porch, under which I proposed to shelter. Then I scooped and stamped and shoveled with hands and feet until I had a spot beneath it all but clear of snow.

Now I was out of the wind, and I sat upon my bundle of belongings and looked at the wall of stone before me. I envisioned a vortex of whirling stone fragments, deep in the face of the rock wall that sheltered me. I spun them like a whirlwind, seeing within myself the beginning of a reddish glow as the friction increased. And when I withdrew my sight from the odd dimension into which it had looked, the wall was glowing with a cherry-red, rippling wave of heat.

Then I laid the large piece of blanket that had substituted for my cloak at a comfortable distance from that comforting warmth, arranged the softer portions of my burden to serve as a pillow, rolled into the blanket, and fell into sleep.

Toward dawn, the wall began to cool enough to let the chill of the plain seep into my nook, and I woke. There in the shelter of the stone, I ate and drank and repacked my gear. And as the sun lightened the cloud-muffled east, I set out across those icy wastes toward the invisible mountains that I knew were awaiting me.

It was a journey to try the endurance of a demon. In summer, I had crossed that expanse of country in less than a week, even afoot. Now I found day melting—no, *not* melting . . . congealing, perhaps?—into day, all progress lost in a blur of snow or a biting rasp of wind fit to freeze the ears from my skull. Still, my infallible sense of direction kept my face to the east, as I could see when, for short whiles, the air cleared enough for the frozen bulks of mountains to appear on the horizon.

It was with relief that I found myself descending into the cleft of the river that meandered down the center of the plain. How many days I had taken to travel that relatively short distance, I have no idea. The shelter of the steep cut was welcome, and the warm springs that bubbled from the rock, just downstream from my point of entry, provided comfort that I had almost forgotten existed.

When I had arranged my camp and eaten enough to take the edge off the gnawing in my belly, I lay on my blanket-cloak and rested, watching the steam billow away up the cleft, which here was very narrow at the top, situated in a bend which made the opening act something like a chimney. My father and I had camped here many times, after hunting the horned ones that grazed the grasslands. The mystery of the hot springs that came out of the earth had fascinated me.

I could hear the voice of Grom, who had always accompanied our hunts, even though he was far too old for the duties of official huntsman, saying, "Aye, a city it was, lying on the plain all in a silken glory, just here. The river, ye mind, flowed in a curve t'other way about, holding that city in its arm, like. They was powerful folk, aye, and rich beyond what king or wizard can claim to be, nowadays, and wicked enough for ten cities. Or so my ma'am and her ma'am, back as far as tale can carry, claimed.

"They carried on trade with nations that be now gone into the dust, and as they waxed fat, their neighbors, far over the mountains, waxed envious. War in those bygone days, the tales say, was no matter of blade and bow and witchery as we know. Strange weapons they must have had, and powerful spells or suchlike that could rend the earth to its deeps. So when an end came to the city of the plain, it was sudden and unexpected, and it smashed that great, comfortable, lazy city into dust and fire.

"Here, just here, mind, it stood, so they say. And it was melted and split and shorn away in one instant, and the river was filled in where it had always curved, and a new channel ran down the terrible split that came in the ground. And, so they say, the city's death still burns like a sickness, deep below. Even if the hot waters didn't stink of foul things, it would be death to drink here."

I could see him sitting there, wreathed in the smelly steam, gazing moodily at the welling-up of the water. I knew, even through my weariness, the uncanny feeling I had always had in this place, and I knew that Grom had felt it even more deeply than I. A thought came, unbidden, into my mind. In such a place the Warlock's powers might well be great. Treachery and death were his own true instruments, and this was, more than any I knew, a spot where both had ruled.

But weariness can reach a point beyond which one cannot drive the flesh, and to such a pass I had come. I must rest, and rest here, where I might expend no effort to warm stones, further depleting my energies. There was no need of covering, so I lay atop my cloak and pillowed my head again on my pack. But I set a guard, nevertheless, that nothing untoward might steal upon me unaware.

It was well that I did, for that unsleeping sense woke me, just as darkness was making the riverbed a cavern of night. I was on my feet before I was aware that I had wakened, my sword in one hand, dagger in the other. I could hear nothing, but I knew with certainty that enemies were approaching down the riverbed.

Soundlessly, I took my belongings and slipped away ahead of them, still downstream, puzzling as I went how it might be that I was now beset, for I knew that neither man nor demon could have tracked me across the plains in that continuing blizzard that had enwrapped me all the way from the western slopes. Only wizardry could have traced me here, and only two were known to me who had powers that might encompass such a task. Varil I trusted as my life. So it was the Warlock who stalked me with his henchmen.

Some breath of my intent as I stood in that distant cleft must have reached across the frozen miles to warn him of my coming.

I stowed my pack and marked in my mind its location. Then I scouted cautiously downstream. And from that direction, too, men were coming. I could hear the grating of rock under booted heels and the occasional splash as someone stepped into the river, which was at this point still unfrozen because of the hot springs just upstream.

I backtracked to the spot where I had left my pack in a deep cleft where a buttress of stone bulged out into the river's cut, narrowing it to a stone's throw across the water, and reducing the rocky edge on which one must travel this deep and swift waterway to the width of two men, elbow-to-elbow. It was the best—and only—defended spot I could find, there in the dark with only years-old memories to guide me. And there I waited.

Those downstream were much nearer than those upstream, so I took a position just behind the buttress of rock, as I heard their approach. I could have cut down the first few without warning, but that smacked of the War-lock's methods, and I had never slain an unwary man. So I stepped out and shouted, "Guard yourselves!" in my loudest voice. And then I was among them. In my position, I could not afford too much good-sportsmanship.

It was all blind hewing and thrusting, and I blessed my two-edged, sharp-pointed weapon, as its star-steel struck sparks from metal helms and sliced through chain-mail throat veils. I had an advantage, there in the darkness. I knew that anyone and everyone was an enemy. They had no way of knowing friend from foe, and the confusion gave me leeway that I used well, while it lasted. For they had neither time nor opportunity to light their torches, which they had extinguished for fear of warning me of their coming.

But my time wore away quickly, for I saw a glimmer growing on the wall across the stream, and I knew that the other contingent was coming at a run from upstream. A dark bulk rose out of shadow and cried, "There he is! Now we can see him!" and came for me with a chopping motion that I was hard put to avoid, as the pain in my side suddenly returned with stunning force. Still, I ducked aside and slid under his guard, stabbing for the join between his helm and his chest plate.

But now the torchlight grew brighter, and four axemen stalked me. I slipped back toward the slit in the rock where my pack lay, and when I reached it two of my attackers were moaning over stumps, while the hands that had grown there still clung to axes that now lay on the ground. The other two, knowing me to be well and truly trapped, drew back to wait for reinforcements, and I took the opportunity to edge into the crack. It might buy a bit of time—or it might let them skewer me like a caged quall. Still, it was all that I knew to do. And as I went through, Varil's voice again whispered inside my ear.

"Go deeper, Karas. It is not so limited as it looks. Go down into the deeps, though that means that I will no longer be able to sense you. But it also means that the Warlock cannot. Find a way, Karas! These lands were so split and shaken in long-past aeons that mazes of crannies run through all the rock, high and low, and you can find a way there. Farewell!"

Outside the cranny, I could hear a babble of voices, moans and howls of pain and rage, and the ominous clinking of many weapons. Anger boiled within me, but it was not at these vermin, who were only tools, guided and promised reward by my enemy. The Warlock would see me yet, and not with the warning that his far-seeing sense might have given him.

I caught up my pack and pushed it ahead of me, as I dropped to crawl along the pebble-floored crack. My body blocked off any ray of light that might have trickled through from the torches outside, so I felt my way blindly, trusting to whatever demon or god or trend of luck had taken me in charge. And the crevice widened. I was able to move forward with my shoulders straight, instead of slanted, one forward and one back. Then I felt space above me, as my movements began to echo hollowly and my ears sensed a changed pressure.

At last I stood and took up my pack, strapping it again on my back. Facing the wall, I ran my hands over it, and then I turned about and took a cautious step. The other wall was there, about an arm's length away. So I faced forward between them, set a hand on each wall lightly, and moved slowly into the deeps of Lantirion.

Soon, the left-hand wall moved out of reach. As I had passed several sharp elbow bends, I felt free to kneel by my pack and kindle my little sun. Only the kings of Lantirion and those of their line have the ability to activate those wondrous things, and I had treasured mine since first my father had given it to me, when I was twelve. It had required no teaching. I knew at once to look deep into it, to agitate its internal particles until they burned with white splendor, and to set a corner of my mind to keeping it aglow. Now I blessed the small chunk of smooth crystal in my hand, as I envisioned it, whirling its atoms to cold flame.

With that inexhaustible light in my hand, I stood and looked about the long corridor in which I now stood. I had never liked the roots of the world, deep places being a matter of discomfort to me. And now I walked through a crack in the cellar of Lantirion, askew from its violent making, dusty and rocky and strewn with rubble still from that ages-forgotten catastrophe that had split the rock and destroyed the city above. I didn't like it, but I set my face forward and moved along it, knowing, with that internal lodestone of mine, exactly how far it was causing me to deviate from a direct course toward the Warlock.

Through the Seeking Sense of Varil

The Warlock stood in his study. Before him the fan shape of the sole window bowed outward above the sheer drop into the valley below the Citadel. It seemed that he stared through darkness across the low country toward the range of mountains beyond.

His eyes, however, were glazed and unseeing. Sweat stood on his forehead, and his face was ridged with effort, his body tense as a bowstring. He had stood thus for hours upon hours, as he flung the quall, like some weird weapon, at the throat of his enemy.

Now he was wearying. On that distant eminence, Karas Lantir swung a dripping blade, and quall piled at his feet in seemingly endless windrows. Still the Warlock strove with the dim and multitudinous minds of the vermin, feeling them diminish in number as he drove them. In the midst of his efforts, he had no strength for physical seeing. Only through the senses of those he guided to their deaths could he perceive some semblance of the battle on that spot.

And suddenly he found himself swept away, as if by wind, to fall with his instruments into darkness . . . almost into death, but he pulled his sensing frantically clear before the moment of impact. Not even vicariously did he want to experience the final mystery.

He recovered himself slowly, looked at the dark sky, the table beside him. Then he shook himself and reached for the wine flagon, poured hastily, and drank. Fortified, he tried to seek outward again.

He had an uncomfortable intuition that only the quall had died. He felt Karas Lantir standing in that distant cleft of rock. He sensed the look of hatred that stretched *like a thread beyond the reach of eyes into the limitless vision of the heart.*

Yet he could not look across those leagues for himself. He had drained all his energies for many days to come in his generaling of the quall.

He could only guess, and his guesses were of bitter defeat. The son of Lantir was tough, yes, and skilled at warfare and sudden death. He was also infernally lucky, and the Warlock clenched his fist in frustration. He would have slammed it onto the reddish wood of the table, but he found himself suddenly too weary to bother.

He touched a velvet cord, and somewhere a deep chime sang once. His servant came quivering into the study, his eyes terrified, as always.

"Yes, Lord King," he said, with the required obeisance.

"See to my bath. Warm my bed. Have the cooks make an omelette. And send Eliar to me."

Without a word, the man backed from the chamber and hurried down the passage, the click of his heels dying into the distance. The Warlock grinned. His malnourished soul relished such outward indications of his power.

In only seconds, another tread, heavier and more certain, thudded toward the door, and a burly man in leather armor entered. His bow was only a jerk of the chin downward.

That seemed to irk the Warlock, but he shrugged his irritation aside and said, "You, Eliar, are the most skilled of all the men at my command. You are experienced in war, ruthless in everything I command you to do. The time has come for me to try my best weapon against this accursed Lantir."

Eliar's face, expressionless as wood or stone, did not change, but he asked, "The old one? He's gone to earth somewhere in the high places. No way to winkle him out before spring."

"Not the onetime King of Lantirion, you fool! His son, who skulks about from hill to plain, talking secretly with those who are disaffected, plotting with those who would see me overthrown. His son, who is . . . or seems to be . . . leagued with demons, so difficult is he to come upon."

The soldier's face did not show any ripple of feeling, but into his eyes flicked a momentary glint of amusement. Not all of those who had chosen freely the service of the Warlock were fools. Most were simple opportunists, as was he, and they laughed together, at times, over the delusions held by that great sorcerer.

His musings were interrupted by the voice of his master.

"Take men—decide for yourself how many will be necessary—and go westward across the plains. They are deep in snow. I know this, for I arranged that they should be. However, I require that you reach the cut of the great river in no more than four days. Lantir will turn eastward, now. I feel it. I know it. He is coming hitherward, and he means my death.

"How long it will take for him to reach the river I cannot gauge, for I do not know how severely he is injured. The injuries, however, will not stop him, or slow him overlong. The snow will be only a hindrance to him. You must be in the river's canyon long before he arrives. We cannot know where he will intersect its length, so you must divide your force, sending men to watch both upstream and down. And you must, you must, you MUST kill him there and drop him down some crevice of stone, bury him beneath a slide of rock, conceal him in some way so that none may know whether he lives or is dead.

"*Eliar, I require this of you.*"

Eliar blinked once. By no other sign did he show that he understood that his life would be the price of failure. When one served corrupt masters, it was often so. But the pickings were fat, while they lasted, and Eliar had no doubt of his own ability to bring Lantir down.

"It will be done, Lord King," he grunted, slapping his metaled heel against the smooth stone of the floor. "I will take twenty. That should be far more than enough, but it is better to be long than short, in work of this kind."

The Warlock nodded dismissal, and the man turned on his heel and left the room in time to jostle the servant as he waited for permission to enter.

When the omelette had been consumed, with a fair wine, the bath taken, and the warmed bed caressed his weary limbs, the Warlock lay for a time in deep thought. Though he was lapped in warmth and luxury, secure in his impenetrable fortress on the knees of a great peak, yet he felt terrible unease.

"Lantir comes," he whispered into the still room. He shuddered, making the huge couch shake and its curtains quiver. Then he sat and drew a shawl about his shoulders, motioning a light into being with a careless finger gesture.

In the loneliness of his chamber, he looked at the fat book that lay on the table at his bedside. Then he took it into his lap, turning the pages of his own tight script as he scanned the lines.

Satisfied at last, he returned the book to its place and quenched the light with another sweep of his hand.

Lying back onto his high pillows, he sighed with pleasure.

"I have planned well," he said to the bed curtain. "Even now, those from Krel are moving through the lands. Soon the vermin of Lantirion will be so occupied with their own problems that they will find no time to be concerned with those of the whelp of Lantir.

"Only I could have conceived so efficient a plan. In the turmoil that will follow the work of the Krel, I will be forgotten by my enemies. And those few who are left to dwell in Lantirion will pose no threat to me."

With another sigh, he turned on his side, and soon deep breaths bore him into sleep.

CHAPTER 3

Scrambling about in the bowels of the world may be a grimy and miserable thing, but at the very least it is free of snow. In fact, it was warm in those deeps, compared to the cold-locked plains above. And, though enemies might well abound here, they would be no instruments of the Warlock, or so I surmised.

After a long time I sat amid the rubble and ate, slowly, of my small store. My water I was even more sparing of, knowing that it might be long before I came again to the surface. What streams had run here, long ago, might well have been blocked away by the shifting of the land, and I did not depend on finding water below ground. Then I let my light dwindle to a spark, and I slept, without guard or caution.

For too long, I had driven my flesh past the wont of wisdom, and the time had come for me to rest completely. I had heard no sound in these deeps except for the echoes of my own passage and the infinitesimal shiftings of the stone. Now I recovered some of the lost energy I had expended so recklessly over the past days.

There was no reckoning how long I slept. I woke with a clear head and a heart that said, "Now we can go on to do our task!" Even the weight of the lands over my head did not depress me as it had in other times.

Again I ate, sparingly but with appetite, and then I scrubbed away the blood and the tension-sweat of the battle I had fought. Handfuls of gritty dust sufficed for the task, and, though they left my skin feeling a bit flayed, I was glad to be rid of the stench of blood.

Refreshed as much as might be, I again took up my journey, finding, to my relief, that there were many branchings off the principal crevice that I had followed. I took, each time, the branch that drew me nearer in the direction of the eastern mountains, and I found before long that I was able to keep my bearing on the Warlock, merely "tacking" back and forth as do the mariners of Krel, in order to gain their direction against an untoward wind.

My many shallow cuts and bites and bruises were a nuisance, as the newer ones scabbed and stiffened and cracked loose and bled afresh, each time I was forced to climb rockfalls or to leap down steep faces too sheer to climb. But I was healing rapidly, I found, even grimed as I was with dust and grit. It may be that the constant temperature aided in this, for I found that the underground remained always the same . . . too chill for comfort but not cold enough for distress.

Still, I made good progress. And in the resting-times I practiced the odd gift that Varil had pointed out to me. I moved things with my mind, watching by the hard, cold light of the little sun as a pebble rolled to my will across the cavern floor or a hanging fragment, high above, loosed itself and flew away down the tunnel and out of sight. Those of my line have always been gifted with such abilities, though we have never made much of them. It was, perhaps, partly because of them that my folk were chosen to rule, in days of old. Their mastery of battle and bloodshed gained them power, and their mastery of weirdities gained them awe. The combination is a rare one and worth holding.

We were not wizards. No dark lore or sorcerous learning was ours, and we scorned such, along with those who used them. They were the shifts of inadequate souls who did not dare to take their fates into their two hands, trusting in the gods, and to shape them to their wills. We merely held an odd gift that ran with our blood through the generations of Lantir. Now I proposed to set them, with my good arms and hard head, against the Warlock himself. So I practiced, and it grew easier and easier to move pebbles, then rocks, then boulders to my command.

I slept again, deep in the heart of my people's kingdom, and walked again, threading my way toward the east, blind as a rat in a wall, but as knowing of my direction. And it seemed to me that I was going deeper into the rock. Each climb was smaller, each descent was longer. A rounded pebble would roll forward from my foot until some obstacle caught it. The weight of all the planet seemed to lie over me, and I turned my thoughts from that, whenever they strayed to it.

There came a time (day and night had lost meaning for me) when I moved into a crack that seemed to lead directly eastward. Holding the little sun high in my left hand, my sword in my right, I walked out of the dead spaces of the random cracks where I had moved for so long . . . into a chamber so large that I could see nothing of it but the mosaic floor at my feet and, behind me, the riven wall through which I had entered. But the sight of those alone was enough to stop my breath in my breast.

The stonework was ablaze with glowing colors, worked into patterns of geometric beauty. The wall was a mural —it seemed glazed onto the stone in some unfathomable fashion—showing men and women dancing, working at unguessable tasks, surrounded by coils and webbings of metal and glass, making love, playing in gushing fountains. Being seized by hooded forms and borne below ground. You could see the shrieks of terror frozen in their painted faces.

I moved along the wall, to my left as I faced it. There were chambers with mosaic floor, like the one on which I stood. They were lit by orbs of light suspended from their vaulted roofs, and they were filled with the hooded forms. Their captives filed down the center of one of the depicted chambers, all dressed in white robes that left their heads bare. The next panel showed the figure toward which they moved.

It was crimson-robed, its hood thrown back. The face was older than death, but a grimace of eagerness gave it a grin. It was a wolfish face, lined with terrible markings, for one with eyes to see. And, in that withered visage, I saw the face of the Warlock. The shape of the skull, the miser's ears, the expression of self-will, all were those of the man I knew little, and too well at that.

I stood long before that pictured face. So, the ancestors of the Warlock had been here even before the fall of the city. They were old in evil, then, and while their craft had undoubtedly been crippled by the collapse of their world, their terrible ambitions and the will to achieve them were with us still. I spat on the floor at my feet.

"Forewarned is as good as an ambush," I said to that wicked old demon on the wall. "Knowing what you were will give me a lever against your remaining child." I turned and walked out into the chamber, my heels ringing defiantly against the patterned floor.

Raising my little sun as high as possible, I looked upward until I saw the orb that hung from the roof just above me. I gazed at it, willing it to glow. And it began to shine, dimly at first, then more strongly until the entire thing burst into splendor.

That section of the chamber leaped into being, and I

stood rooted as I looked about me. There are devices that outlaws use to wrest from victims the hiding places of their treasures. Such things are themselves outlawed. Here were devices that made those look like cradles for the comforting of babes. And along the walls were graphic scenes showing them in use.

My neck hair rose with revulsion and fury. Recklessly, I ignited the remaining orbs, until the entire chamber stood revealed, as it must have been in the days of its glory. After one more glance, I looked no more upon the walls. The torture of many is no more sin than that of one, as any such is an affront to the gods, as well as to those of human kind.

As I stood there, I heard sounds . . . shufflings and whisperings and titters . . . coming from the far end of the chamber, where a half-wall protected an obscene altar. Unsheathing my sword and taking my dagger in my left hand, I stalked grimly down the length of that unholy chamber and through the arched opening in the low wall.

Creeping from low doorways in the curving wall, from behind the reddish stone of the altar, from along the wall itself came a throng of half-human figures. Slumping, crawling like beasts, they still had the shapes of men and women, though they were overgrown with coarse hair that had taken the place of clothing. And they were white —albino white, even to their staring and sightless eyeballs. They were also armed. Rusted bits of metal in their hands held, here and there, the hint of spear shape or of sword. Some bore clubs that were evidently cobbled up from ancient fittings of this unholy temple to man's worst traits. All carried something, and all moved toward any sound I made, pausing only when I stood still, scarcely breathing.

They moved soundlessly, and I shuddered to think of

the ages these last inheritors of this terrible place must have spent in preying upon chance rodents—and worse, one another—in the dark of this noisome den. One let his weapon clink against the altar, and those nearest were upon him in one pounce. And then I learned how they continued to go on, generation after generation. Before they killed him (and one another) they ran their hands over him to determine his sex. All but one of the hideous crew died, one way or another, in that small and silent battle, and the survivor, forgetting his original task, settled down to feast on what remained.

I walked through that temple, and the rooms and corridors beyond, and I killed all I met. Without compunction I slew them, helpless as they were against one with sight. I hunted out their warrens, and I killed and killed until my blades both ran red. Females heavy with young died before me, and older ones who were agile enough to survive the attentions of their children. I killed the rodent-stinking infants lying in nests of filthy litter. When I was done, the place was filled with their corpses, but it felt cleaner.

I stood, at last, in the great chamber of the temple, and I turned toward the altar. My fury had not yet waned, and I cried in the greatest voice I could muster, "You, profanity of profanities who, under guise of godhead, led the fathers of these wretches into darkness, I sentence to eternities of darkness. No acolyte is left to you, not even the least of those wretches who have amused your loneliness in these few past ages. Nothing to worship you! Nothing to fear you! Nothing to drag before you a shrieking rat or a weeping being from the world of sunlight! I leave you alone!"

One by one I extinguished the orbs that glowed on high. As I reached the next to last, there came a sighing sound from the now-darkened end of the temple. I looked, and the horrible altar crumbled quietly into dust as I watched. With a smile, I put out the last of the great lights and, using my little sun, picked my way across that awful black gulf to the crack in the farther wall that matched the one through which I had come. I entered the clean randomness of natural things with relief.

But I didn't pause to rest for many miles, and I picked my way along tunnels and crannies, through slits and among spaces filled with rubble, with something like joy to be again among the things of the gods. Not until I could no longer feel behind me the contamination that was the temple where the Warlock's longfather had ruled did I pause to clean myself again with dust.

Then it occurred to me that somewhere in that filthy warren there must have been a stream or well that supplied the needs of those who had lived there. But I was as well content . . . nothing would have induced me to drink anything that they had befouled. I sipped from my tiny supply of brackish water, and it tasted sweet as a spring brook, even mixed as it was with wine.

CHAPTER 4

I slept twice again underground, but I could now feel that I was moving toward the surface again. My climbs grew longer, descents shallow and few. And there came a time when I moved into a draft of icy-fresh air that smelled of snow and fir trees. Some chimney in the rock was drawing the air from another crevice, through the black tunnels in which I had walked for so long.

I searched for many hours, but the openings must have been very narrow and well-hidden, for I never found anything into which I could have crawled. So I went eastward again, and at last I came to a bore that had been the channel of some long-dried stream. Down its tube came a blast of cold wind, and I knew that I had found my way out of the deeps. Following that relatively smooth way, I came out into the upper air again.

I was in a crack in the side of a bluff. Below me was a slope of fir-covered hill, deep in snow. I retreated into the shelter of the underground ways again for long enough to unpack my furs and wrap myself well against the chill. Then I strapped the pack tightly to my back and made my way out onto the bluff face and down, handhold to foothold to crevice to ledge, to the foot of the bluff.

A stream, deep-locked in ice, pooled in a wide curve, nearby, and I broke through and filled my bottle with the tooth-crackingly cold water and drank sparingly of it. My food pouch was empty, as it had been for about a day, and

I next looked for game trails in the snow. There were tracks of all kinds, and I chose those of a pair of tallow-birds, knowing that their all-but-useless wings and short legs would make them easy prey.

The snow was light and new-fallen, which made it easy to move quietly after my would-be meal. When I saw their trail all kicked and dusted with scratchings, I dropped to my belly and crawled forward, keeping my head well down. While the brain of the tallow-bird is small, its eyes are keen. But I managed to creep near enough to the bush under which they were sheltering so that, when I hurled a snowball to land just on its other side, the two rushed, preeping with alarm, directly into my hands. With a bird in each hand, I rose and bore my flapping burden up into the sheltering deeps of the fir wood.

A goodly way into the wood, I found a ledge of rock over which a big fir had fallen recently enough that the needles were still clinging to its boughs. Against the waist-high wall of rock, beneath the tent of fir branches that had kept the ground clear of snow, I went to earth. Wringing the necks of the birds, I built a fire, using the mat of dried twigs and needles underfoot to kindle larger, wetter wood to a blaze. I kept the fire small, not wishing to attract any observer's attention; what with the bounty now laid on my head, I little knew what the folk would do, if they knew that I was by.

When the fat was dripping lazily into the coals from the spitted birds, I sat against the rock, listening to the snow-melt from my "roof" hissing onto the fire. And as I sat, I thought of Varil. Though I knew that I might thereby bring the attention of the Warlock again in my direction, I gazed into the flame and called her name, deep inside myself.

The coals glowed white in the center, red-orange about

the edges. In the center of their shimmer, an image grew, and Varil looked out at me, her eyes sleepy and surprised. Her bright hair was tumbled about her shoulders, and I could see a wisp of her night robe over one white shoulder.

"Karas?" she whispered, and her eyes widened. She yawned and rubbed away sleep with her knuckles, like a child. "Karas? Where are you?" Then she held up a hand. "Don't tell me. The Warlock might know of it."

I laughed at her. "What do you, sleepyhead? Here in midafternoon you are still abed!"

She yawned again, then smiled. "I wearied away the night seeking for you, Karas Lantir! I felt you nearing the surface, after being lost to my senses for these many, many days. All the night I sought for you, but you must have been still underground."

"If you sensed me so, has the Warlock also, think you?" I asked with concern.

"The Warlock, my chuck, has not shared your heart, your mind, and your bed. There are some closenesses that surpass wizardry, let the wizards rage as they will. And, know it for truth, your image has altered, in your time below ground. Even your face has changed, and your stance. That seal of self that you send abroad for those who have the internal eye to see has grown and widened and become other than it was. I think that the Warlock will believe that a rival has entered his lands secretly. He will not suspect that you are the newcomer he senses."

"Have I changed enough that the folk may not know me for Lantir?" I asked her.

"You are bearded, and your beard is black where before it was darkest brown, though you kept it so close-shaven that none but your dearest knew. Your hair is now darker and streaked with gray. I might not have known you, even I, had I met you by chance on the road," she answered. "I long to know the tale of your passage of the underways. That must wait, I fear, many a long day. But that journey has changed you so that your own father, so I believe, would greet you as a stranger."

"Then I may go with less wariness among the folk of the hills," I mused. "That will make things easier."

"Take care that you do not betray yourself!" she warned. "You were much given to faring abroad with your subjects, be they high or low. A chance word in the wrong ear could be of much danger. But I trust your wisdom. By the look of you, you have won through far more perilous things . . . and totally without my aid!" She smiled ruefully, and I laughed, knowing the strangely protective feeling she had toward me, who was large enough to lift her in one hand.

A branch broke in a shower of sparks, and the vision faded. I lay back against the rock and dozed away the afternoon, waking now and again to replenish the fire, or to eat a bit more of the birds. When darkness fell, it was no true night, for the snow-glimmer made every object stand out as if etched in soot against the pristine whiteness. Then I broke down a branch, letting a rush of heavy snow cover all trace of fire and occupancy. Taking my diminished pack, I slipped along the ledge, setting my feet in line under its sheltering lip so that no track sullied the snow. As it angled away around and up the slope, it suited me well.

I came at last to an overarching tree whose limbs swept down into my reach, and I swung myself up and hand over hand along one until I came well away from the ledge I had followed. Then I dropped into a thorny bush, extricated myself from it with curses and scratches, and set off to climb the hill to its top, in order to get my bearings, for the lands that I knew like my own garden in summer were much changed now beneath snow.

As I reached the crest of the hill, moving cautiously among the thickets of young conifers that had grown up where some past fire had raged, I froze to stillness. Voices sounded ahead of me, and one was a familiar one. I listened closely as the men drew near. They chatted carelessly, and the familiar voice drew to itself a name.

Shal . . . aye, it was Shal. Whatever god—or demon—arranges the game of chance that is life had sent into my path one with whom I had played as a child in these hills. Shal I would trust with my life in battle or hunt. But caution was a word not in his vocabulary. What came into his mind came forth in words without finding a path through his brain. He would withstand torture in order not to betray me, and the next moment he might well call me by name, from sheer absentmindedness.

Still, so the dice fell, and I knew that I must play out the blind game that I had been playing since leaving the dead quall on the distant mountain to the west. So I stepped forward steadily, as though I had walked without pause up the slope. Emerging from the stand of young trees, I found myself less than thirty paces from the men I sought.

Shal looked at me carelessly, then closely, and then he said in his direct, undeceivable, childlike way, "Ho, Karas! A strange time you pick to hunt in the high country. You should be whiling away these gray days with your mistress!"

It was just as well that I had said nothing to try to befool him. Both nettled and amused, as always, by his unique ways, I said, "Why Shal, know you not that there is a ban laid on me throughout Lantirion? You might be sent to torture and death, merely for pausing to speak to me on the trail. And your companion may wish to avail himself of the reward the Warlock has offered for my—detached—head."

A shout of laughter went up. The shorter of the two came up to me and took my mittened hand in both of his own. "Hru Karas," he said, using the antique form of address that the hill people alone still clung to, "we are of Lantir, here. None who walk these heights pays heed to the maunderings of wizards. And I, too, though you do not remember me, was once a playfellow. I am the grandson of Grom, and you dandled me on your knee when you were a stripling and I a babe."

I looked at his fresh young face, red with snow-chill, with merry dark eyes and youthfully sparse blond beard. Somewhere in that adult countenance, I could see a vestige of that well-remembered infant that had given me such delight in the long evenings we had spent in Grom's lodge, after a day of hunting. I went forward and grabbed both in a bear hug, grateful to feel again the contact of warm human flesh, after the long days of cold wandering among dire things.

Laughing, we went away down the hill together to their village, and I helped them carry the slung carcass of a horn-beast that they had killed in the twilight. The firelight glinted red through the chinks around doors and shutters, and after we had hung the gutted game in the meat house, I welcomed the chance to lie once again within walls, before a crackling hearth fire.

Shal led me to his own home, and I was astonished to think that he had grown up, as had I, and now had his own wife and two toddling young ones. Remi, his wife, welcomed me with the forthright lack of coquetry that I had always liked about hill women. She set before us a pot of savory stew and two long-handled ladles and left us to our own devices, while she washed the babes and made them ready for bed.

It took no long time for us to fill our bellies (almost emptying the pot in the process), and soon we were basking upon the skins laid before the hearth. There, Remi brought to us the children to be fondled and kissed. They were delightful babies, warm and sweet from their scrubbing, wrapped in hooded and footed fur coveralls that allowed them to sleep unencumbered, even in the cold of winter.

Tul, the boy, was older by a year than his sister, Relya. Their button-bright eyes were full of intelligence and mischief, and I knew that before long they would have me as firmly enthralled as Grem, Grom's grandson, had in days long gone. There was a fine tussle and much laughter, there before the fire, and when Remi herded them firmly off to bed I felt a regret to see them go.

But Shal and I had grimmer things to talk of. Without hesitation, I told him of my banning and the bounty and the hounding by quall and by men that I had undergone. The tale of my journey underground made his brown eyes widen and his ruddy cheeks pale, for nothing holds more terror for a hillman than the thought of entrapment.

When I finished my story, he sighed a long breath. Then he said, "Karas, while you hid beyond the western mountains, and while you have been making your way hitherward, ill things have fallen on our lands and our folk. Many protested your banning. Many of those disappeared, not to reappear. When the bounty was proclaimed, there was outcry, even in the capital city of Antri, where all know that men know little of loyalty. (I let this pass, for I knew of the long history of misconception and dislike between those of the city and those of the hills and farms that supported it.)

"Twenty were seized from their homes and their shops and hanged, women as well as men, those under the age of reason as well as those older. The land is on the brink of revolt, and armed men move by night along every road and trail that is passable, though the bitter winter has slowed that traffic to a trickle. And yesterday Hral, the half brother of Grem, returned from taking the last load of furs to Antri, and he brought terrible news . . . or rumor that seems to have the weight of news.

"They say that the Warlock has given leave to the slavers of Krel to prey upon the folk of Lantir, so long as they dare to raise any voice against the things he does."

I stood, in one motion, and, almost, a roar of rage found its way from my throat, but I thought of the children and forebore. Shal raised his hand and motioned me down again.

"There is worse," he said. "Though that rumor seemed the raving of madmen, and Hral gave it little credence, on his way back here he passed through two villages that had been peaceful and untroubled when he went forth. Now they lie broken-doored and empty, and the winter wind alone finds voice there. None remained in either to tell him what their fate was. But we fear . . . we fear!"

I looked up into his eyes, as he sat erect on the skins, and the feckless Shal I knew as a boy seemed only a dim memory. A man sat there, one who had given hostages to chance and was sorely beset with worry for the next days, or even hours. He looked toward the split-log door.

"No bear can force my door," he said, echoing my thought. "But men with rams can, or men who do not hesitate to set fire to the roof can force us out into the arms of slavers. I sit here before my own fire, and I feel the approach of wickedness. Is it only my fear, or is it something real that comes toward us through the snow?"

"Let me find Varil," I said. "She will be able to far-see. My small talents do not include that useful gift."

So I gazed again into flames, and my lady began to take shape in their glow. "You call me again so soon?" she asked. "Surely, I must feel flattered."

But I cut off her badinage with, "Varil, I sit before the hearth of Shal, my brother in all but blood. We feel the approach of black evil. Yet I cannot look abroad, as you do, to find if it is real. Will you work your magics for us, for Shal has wife and small ones. We fear for them."

Her glimmering face grew sober at once, and she seemed to turn her eyes inward. Then they flashed out at me with urgency and horror. "Go," she cried. "Stop for nothing, but take those in your care to safety. The Warlock's men are all but at the door!"

And with that word, Shal and I leaped to action, Shal running into the loft for Remi and the children, and I to the kitchen for a quick sweep of loaves and dried meat into a bag. We caught weapons from the walls as we went by, and before the branch had broken from which Varil had looked at us, we had Remi and the young ones out a back window of an unlighted room.

Remi had long had emergency supplies of bedding and warm clothing prepared, for she and Shal knew that his old friendship with me might well bring about their own banning. So they went into the snowy wood with supplies enough for a time. And she led the toddlers away through the snow to a long-arranged hiding place that Shal had found and stocked with firewood. We watched them out of sight, but it had begun to snow again and that was soon, indeed. It was good, for it wiped away their trail.

Then Shal and I ran down into the village and tapped urgently at windows, rousting forth Grem and his family to help us warn the rest. Before we reached the last hut, we could hear a muffled uproar from Shal's home, and we knew that the baffled slavers were searching for whoever might be hiding there. But they were doomed to disappointment, for we got all the village out into the snow and away, long before they approached the rest of the houses.

There was no family that did not have its secret hiding spot, for the past year of living under the rule of the Warlock had not given them any sense of security in their lives. Most had stocked caves or huts built secretly, high in the foothills, and to those shelters the families were sent.

CHAPTER 5

Grem and Shal and I remained to watch the actions of the slavers, serving as a sort of rear guard for those who were fleeing. But I had other purposes, also. Though I said nothing to the others, I was sickened by the thought of those two villages of my folk who were even now, more than likely, shackled and hidden away by the henchmen of this wicked crew. I did not intend that they should long remain the captives of these men.

When the slavers had hallooed and burst open unlocked doors and battered in shutters enough to tire them, they gathered in the small clearing that centered the village and held a conference of sorts. In the now-thickening fall of snow, we were able to creep very near, but they were jabbering in a tongue I could not recognize even as one of the dialects of Krel. I surmised that they had been recruited from an even less civilized nation to do the filthy tasks that lined the pockets of the canny Krel—and the Warlock. If I knew him at all, he was not simply using the slavers to quell my people. He was growing wealthy through their sale.

My very bones were shaken by the depth of my rage, but I contained it (as I had not been able to do, just a short span of days before) and thought on my next step. Turning to my friends, I said, "Now that the folk are safe, you can go to your own families and see to their safety and comfort. I must follow these beasts and find where they hold those others they captured."

But Shal laughed softly, and Grem grunted. "Think you that we, too, do not cringe to think of our neighbors held by those less-than-men?" demanded Shal. "Remi is no softling. I pity any who might come upon her lair with intent to do harm to her or to the children. He would not come out again. They are as safe as one can be in this unchancy world. Grem's parents are guarded well by sons and daughters. Others would join us in a moment . . . indeed, they asked us if they might not aid you, for all of us guess what you intend. A Lantir could do no other. But we whispered to them that this was a task fit for a few to do. Many might well betray themselves. But we three can take a bear by the tail, if we so choose, without waking him to our presence."

I grinned into the darkness. In truth, Shal had grown into a man whose friendship I might prize more than a kingdom. And Grem was like to do so. Without answering, I tapped Shal on the shoulder and moved into the darkness after the now departing slavers. And, though I heard no faintest hint of sound, I knew that the two were following.

It was not easy, in that ever thickening pall of snow, to keep to their trail, as the slavers moved with the quiet of disciplined troops, rather than with the noise of a rabble. They slipped through that unfamiliar wood as softly as did we, and that told us much about their training and caliber. I revised my earlier opinion. No cutthroat who sells his services for simple slaving could—or would—submit to such stringent discipline. We were tracking soldiers, or I was a weanling. And that would make a great difference in strategy.

We were now following them down into a ravine whose sides angled so steeply beneath our feet that we held onto the thickly growing firs in order to keep from pitching down upon the heads of those we pursued. Far below, I could hear the chuckle of still unfrozen water, and I knew that the stream at the bottom of the cut must be both very swift and extremely well protected by overgrowth from the cold.

Part way down, Shal touched my shoulder and gestured for us to halt. When we no longer had to concentrate on keeping our footing and avoiding the clawing branches, we could hear a dim murmur of voices . . . and the crack of a whip. I heard Grem, on my left, groan unconsciously as the sharp sound died into the muffling snow silence. I put my hand on his arm and squeezed it in sympathy. The sound had raised my own hackles, and I felt the beginning of the red rage that had several times in my life overriden my will and sent me into actions that no sane man would have attempted.

Now we had a notion of the prisoners' location, we knew that we need not try to follow their captors down. We slipped away along the slope, then down to the edge of the stream. It was, indeed, well protected. A veritable tunnel of red-berried bushes arched over the narrow streambed, and the water that moved noisily through was partly iced over. Just above the thickest of the bushes along the way was a game trail so faint and narrow that if Shal and Grem had not known it as well as they knew their own bedchambers it would have been impossible to discern. But it was there, and in its miserly clearance we could approach the encampment of the slavers without haste or risk of being heard.

The camp that they had made for those unfortunate people was little more than a crouching place in the snow, though it was shielded by a bit of overhang from the steep rock that walled in the ravine at that spot. Only one fire burned, and it was a skimpy one, just enough to char a bit of meat and warm the backsides of the slavers. We could hear, even at a distance, the chattering of many sets of teeth, and as we drew near we stumbled over the body of a year-old babe, cast away into the snow like offal.

Then my head began to work again as the head of a prince should. I tapped Grem and pointed upslope. In the darkness, I whispered to him his instructions, and he faded away from sight at little more than arm's length. Shal looked at me, his face almost touching mine in the eery snowlight. He pointed up the path, then brought his hands together. I nodded, and he was away like the shadow of a ghost.

I waited. In a bit I heard the tweeerp! of a startled snowbird from up the hill. That told me that Grem was in position. Shal's progress I knew almost as if I were moving with him, and when I was sure that he had gained the far side of the camp, I heard a terrific shout from Grem shatter the night.

Those we had followed had barely had time to take off their gear and seize a bit of meat from the spit over the fire. The rest were armed but totally unready. They scrambled for helms and swords, dropping food as they moved. But they steadied down quickly and moved away up the slope toward the spot where Grem was making a fine job of sounding like a force of men moving through the trees.

Without uttering the scream that I longed to let free, I shot into the small sheltered place and hissed at the exhausted folk there, "Come! And quietly, for your lives!"

My people are no fools. Even the smallest of them rose to their feet and moved toward me at once, though I could see that some were sorely hurt, and more than one was only borne along by his fellows, being unable to walk. But they moved, and swiftly, down the path toward me. I set them to moving still farther, and turned to the old woman who stood forth and waited to speak to me.

"Adalla?" I asked, unsure, after so many years, whether this wrinkled and stalwart person was the one I remembered from my childhood.

"Aye," she whispered. "And still leader of my folk. Where do I take them?"

"Follow the path along the stream. Some of your hunters may know it, which will be of aid to you. Shal will come after you . . . if the gods will it. If not, take your stand and cost them dearly for every life. Stones and branches were the first weapons and still may make a dent in a man, if used properly."

She moved to touch my face with a wondering paw. "The face is not the same, but the words are the words of Lantir. We go, Lord. Be unworried. None of us will again wear the shackles, unless they chain our corpses." And she followed her people quickly from sight, down the dim twist of the path.

I moved into the place from which I had called them out, and there I found Grem waiting for me, with Shal, who muttered, "I made a great trail upstream. They will think a host has gone that way, if they look to track our folk."

Then we were still, waiting for the return of those who were even now trying to find nonexistent attackers from above. Soon they moved back toward the camp, and those who came first called out to the guards they had left there. But Shal had sent them to endless rest before making his counterfeit trail, and it was left to me to grunt, "Hai!" in answer to their words.

My voice was not to their liking, for they came with a rush, and I let the red fury take me in hand and whirled into a vortex of blood and bright blades glinting in firelight. There were only a dozen in that first group, and the three of us churned through them in a flail of steel and snow and terrible sweat. Then we turned and went back through them, and when we were done not one was on his feet or able to draw breath again.

That, of course, drew the twenty who still searched the slope down to the source of the clamor. They came more cautiously, and we moved into the upstream path and slipped upslope, leaving the trampled trail to mislead them into thinking us a much larger force than we actually were.

They were well led. They came warily, fanned out up the slope, as well as along the track. We crouched and became snow-laden bushes until the last had passed us. Then we quietly cut the throats of those last three in the bunch and moved up to do the same with the next. But we were interrupted.

Up that trail came a group of our own people—we could tell because the chains that had coffled them together still clanked from their wrists. They were armed with the weapons from those we had killed in the camp, and they were not to be stopped. So we rushed with them after the slavers, and we shouted as with one throat to bring them about to face us. They turned in their tracks, as we could see in the now clearing snowlight, and waited for our rush.

Our hunters may not be warriors by trade, but their skills make them the equals of most. These had seen babes and wives and husbands slain or left to die in the snow, and that gave their hands a cunning they might not have had before. The two groups came together, and I was torn between matching steel with those who came before me and trying to look after my raging people. But they didn't need me. As I parried a swinging stroke and slit the man's gizzard with my hand dagger, I saw a young woman just behind him catch a mailed figure with the slack of her chain and break his neck before he could draw back his blade to skewer her.

All around me they were taking vengeance, and I contented myself with occupying the more heavily armed of our opponents. I caught sight of Shal and Grem, now and again, plying their knives with terrible cunning. We were moving farther along the trail and the steep slope, and as I wove about in the melee I could see that we were leaving behind a carpet of bodies to stare at the clearing sky. Dark patches of blood stained the pure snow, and the trees stood root-deep in corpses.

Only when the last of the slavers lay dead did the terrible wrath of the people subside. Then they dropped where they stood, drained of all strength by the ordeal of the past days, hunger, cold, and the force of their anger that had borne them through the battle with their erstwhile captors. It was left to Shal, Grem, and me to go through the victims, one by one, separating friend from foe, giving those who were wounded aid or the coup de grace, our own dying gratefully at our hands.

Our fallen people we gathered into a pile, mercifully a comparatively small one, and heaped it about with deadfall from the wood about us. Shal went down the stream to find the others, and he brought back with him Adalla, whose right it was to set the pyre alight while she chanted the old litany for the dead. She came with him, bowed down by grief for the slaughter of her villagers . . . until she saw the windrows of enemy dead.

Then she lifted up her old voice in a chant of triumph for glorious victory. She took the torch that Shal had lit in the fire at the old camp and stood with it beside the little heap of her friends and kinsmen. We had shaken the snow

from the branches, so that they were fairly dry, and the
smaller twigs at the edges caught with a crisp crackling.
Needles caught up with a soft roar, and Adalla stood,
torch in hand, and watched as the fire mounted.

"Go forth in flame, hillfolk!" she cried in a minor key,
taking up the rhythm of the old ritual. "Where there has
been no ease but toil, no joy but honor, none can protest
his dying. Go forth, now, in the fires of life and death,
bearing with you into the otherworld the weight of your
lives and the honor of your deaths. Go forth in peace,
now, who knew it little in this world. Go forth, and know
that your village and your clan and your kin will remember, while fire casts up smoke, while snow falls on
the hills, while fir trees bear needles, while the waters roll
from high to low. Go forth, go forth in joy!"

The three of us stood in the edge of the circle of light
and raised our voices. "We remember!" rolled away to the
verges of the hills. And from the huddled figures among
the trees came an echo from the weary people, "We
remember!"

By the light of the pyre, we gathered the people together and helped them along the way, moving down the
stream, for Shal said that there was a dry cave farther
downstream, then up the slope a bit to a point where the
hill had cracked, then settled, in ages gone by. So we
crept along until we found that spot, then we hauled up
the wounded and the weary, and we built a great fire in
that grateful shelter. As most of the villagers had only
scanty clothing, that they had caught up when their village was attacked by night, they gathered around and
soaked up the heat, some of them weeping as feeling
began to return to frosted extremities.

Leaving them to rest, Shal and Grem went out to hunt
for a horn-beast, for food was the next pressing need. But

I went back along our old track, for I felt the need to see to the welfare of those we had left behind in Shal's own village hideaways. They little liked to see me go, those two old friends, but they knew that I was compelled by my own fate, subject to my own instincts, in the task I had set out to do, so we parted with a touch of the hands, a touching of cheeks, and the near-dawnlight swallowed us, one by one.

From the memory of Grom

For months, the old king had sat, by day, looking afar over his lost kingdom. By night he slept little, Grom knew, for he could hear him turning and turning upon his sheepskin by the fire. As to eating, the old man had less appetite than an autumn cricket, and his good wild mutton went barely tasted, along with the bannock that Grom knew was the best made in all Lantirion.

Though he was older by a hand-span of years than his lord, Grom was so tough, so weathered-oak strong, that he never thought of himself as old. The king was another matter. Every day that passed, the ex-lord of Lantirion was more bent, more withered, and less able. He was dying by inches, there upon the height where Grom had thought to preserve him in security.

The old huntsman grew dour, when he found that his forced good cheer roused no answering spark in the king. The time came when he, too, sat upon stone and gazed across the Plain, which could be seen through a notch between peaks to west of their aerie. His thoughts were poor company, indeed, as he mulled the twisted skein of events that had led him and his lord to perch like mountain sheep upon a crag too lofty for chance-comers.

He had not dreamed, long ago when he built the small stone hut on this forgotten height, that he might spend the days of his age here. Then he had been restless and venturesome, and this hidden spot had been his fortress. From it he had ventured forth to climb peaks that were thought to be unscalable, in his youthful folly climbing alone, prey to any mischance. He had carried many a wary sheep down from the precipices above and butchered it for his larder. Sitting, bone-weary beneath the many aches of age, he remembered those days as if from the youth of someone else.

Those stolen summers had been all that allowed him to keep his vow of service to his friend and ruler. And even then he had avoided Antri and the court there with every wile he could devise.

The king had shaken his head, when others had complained of his long absences. "I know that you must live in the wild, my friend Grom, or else go mad like a forest creature imprisoned in a cage. Yet I miss your straight tongue and your hard head, when you are not at my side." And so he said to those who thought to displace his chief huntsman and old companion.

And just such a truancy had he been guilty of when the king had most need for him. He had not even the excuse of youth to ease his burden of guilt, for he had been little younger than he was now. A fit of the old hunger had caught him, amid the brash younglings and ignorant courtiers who followed the ruler of Lantirion even into the forest and the Plain. He had longed for escape to the high places, for the clean winds and the unspoiled snows of his old haunt. With leave, he had gone, and in his absence the king had had a visit from the Warlock.

Grom groaned inwardly, taking care that no sound passed his lips. If he had only been in his rightful place, at the king's side, when that wily sorcerer came calling! The addlepates who called themselves the Advisors of

Lantirion had accepted the villain on his own terms, bringing him to their lord as one who wished to tender his loyalty to his ruler. They had allowed him to present a gift of wine, then to share it, amid increasing recklessness and hilarity, with their lord for whom they were responsible.

The thought drove Grom wild with anger. Any ten-year boy, in the mountains, would have known that treachery was afoot. But not those pink-sashed darlings, all spit curls and tin swords, who made such a great thing of being the Royal Guard of Lantirion!

According to the word he had been able to gather, only the young Prince Karas had been wary. He had questioned the Warlock closely, had refused to share his wine. He had spoken sharply to his father, though since his return from his youthful span of wandering and war he had found little to quarrel about.

The very fact that the king had refused to listen to his son should have alerted those who were responsible for his welfare. For Karas had become a man and a soldier. His temper had been subdued so that it served rather than ruled him, and his wit had sharpened to a razor edge. His father had found that more than the comfort of a son had returned with him from his journeying.

Grom had his own thoughts upon the reason for the king's untypical behavior. The hardness of the man's head he knew well, from years of matching cup for cup around the campfires. No common brew or vintage could have so shaken him in his wits.

As to the unlucky throw of the dice, that Grom doubted more than all else combined. He remembered the boy who had been his friend long before the burdens of rule had fallen upon him. And that lad had had an uncanny way with dice—or pebbles—or even arrows in flight. A trick, he would say, laughing. But Grom knew that no cast that bore with it the fate of his kingdom could possibly have gone wrong, if the king had been himself.

So they sat, the two of them, like carrion crows upon a height, and brooded over their own wrongdoings. He had no doubt that the king, even more than he, felt himself to blame for the loss of Lantirion to so unchancy a winner.

Yet Grom knew, also, that their worries were not for two old men, outcast and alone, but for the hapless folk, left in the hands of such a lord. The Warlock had lived for more generations than men could remember in the eastern mountains. The place, as well as the man, had a dark name. And now he had built a Citadel, nearer to the ways tenanted by the people. He had staffed it with strange henchmen who were not folk of Lantirion, and odd tales crept out over the adjacent peaks of the building and delving and going and coming that took place there.

He feared for the people. They had worn the light yoke of the Lantirs for so long that they were unwary and trusting of those who set themselves to rule. It might well be that they would come to grief.

Across the long ways down to the Plain, clouds had gathered, dark-rolled, foretelling snow. A bite in the wind brought Grom to his feet, urging his lord into the hut. Before they reached the door, sharp flecks of blown snow were moving down the air.

Grom fed the low blaze in the hearth from his pile of coal, blessing the outcropping seam that surfaced higher on their peak. By the flickering light, the two warmed a stew of mutton and root-herbs, but the king ate little. When he set aside his bowl, he leaned forward and set his elbows on his knees.

"I have sat here, Grom, for many a month. We have been safe here, as you intended, and I have spent the time *wisely, I think. I have set my mind in order. I have come to terms with my conscience, though that was no easy thing to do. I have remembered, again and again, that day when the kingdom was lost, and I can only conclude that witchery—and worse—were used against me.*

"This does not lessen my guilt, yet it makes the danger of this man more apparent. One who will use deceit in one thing will use it in all, and my folk are unused to being deceived.

"And now something evil moves in the wind. This is no common storm of winter. This is no ordinary snow. It stinks of sorcery, and I fear it. My heart tells me that my people have not been overfond of their new lord, and that he has had scant reverence from them. I feel that he will punish them with terrible things, undeserved miseries that I can only guess at."

"But we'm be only two old crutches," Grom objected. "What c'ld such as we do agin him? We hanna men, or strength, or weapons of pow'r. It be a question if we c'ld get ourseln down fr' this mountain, the now."

"Nevertheless, we must go," said the king. "Whatever happens to my folk, I brought it upon them by my folly. It was madness to give audience to the Warlock. It was worse madness to accept his gift and to drink it. Whatever they suffer, I must be there. To stop it if I can, to suffer with them, if that is all that I can do.

"Get together what we will need, my friend. Tomorrow we must leave our haven and go down. The Citadel he has built is less distant than it might be. Perhaps I will carry the attack to him in his own place."

Grom shuddered. The wind howled against the stone of the walls fit to carry away the hut bodily. They had little warmth left, they two, in their aged carcases, and he had little doubt that that small bit would be wrested from them in the storm.

"We'm lay our bones where none but the sheep and the sun wi' see'm e'er agin," he muttered. But his voice was more cheerful, more alive, than it had been in many a week.

He looked up and saw his master grinning at him. Though the face was wrinkled and weathered, the grin was that of the boy who had been his friend. Grom felt his own face cracking into a matching one.

"Two old gizzards, goin' off to war," he chuckled.

"Should we sit before the fire while the younglings die in our stead?" asked the king, gently. "What war we can manage, that we will achieve, Grom. And if we can but distract the Warlock from his fell purposes, we will do well."

CHAPTER 6

One by one, I sought out the refugees from the village. All seemed well and as comfortable as might be, though wary and hard to come upon without a cut throat or an arrow-pierced body. Remi I found last of all, well situated in a bear's den that she and Shal had enlarged and lined with small, even branches, to make a dry floor. With skins to wrap in, a fire hidden from any eyes and vented so cunningly through a stump hole that even should a marauder smell the smoke, he would never find it, she and the little ones were well, indeed.

Satisfied that all my folk were now out of the hands of the slavers and safe from the attentions of any more Krel that might come looking for the first group, I turned my thought to other villages deeper in the hills. They must have warning. And, more urgently still, the comings and goings of those who hunted my subjects at the behest of the Warlock must be traced, stymied in their efforts, and frustrated in their aims. Though I knew that many would gladly go with me about the task, I felt that it was better suited to one alone, who might move swiftly and silently, and who might with impunity slay any who encountered him, without fearing that it might be one of his own.

So I moved up the ever-rising slopes, after an interval of rest and food with Remi and the children. I watched the snow for strange footprints, I scanned the sky for traces of smoke, and I sniffed the wind for the acrid odor

of men too long in leather and mail. Casting backward
and forward across the rising lands, I found no mark to
show the presence of any alien thing, but I felt, deep
within me, that there were others moving as secretly as I.
As I passed near villages, I sought out woodcutters and
huntsmen and warned them to take their folk into hiding.

I never revealed who I really was, pretending to be one
sent by the lower villages for the warning of their more
remote brethren. Every spot where men dwelled together
in all the hills was engraved upon my memory, for that
was a part of the teaching given any heir of Lantir. My
childhood lessons had made the villages, the wells, the
groves and fields and craft-families as much a part of me
as my own blood and bone, so I lost no time in searching
for settlements. I knew them all.

When I was done, I cast back downward a bit, following the deep burns that cut the ridges with their ravines
and powerful waters. Those had been the sorts of places
chosen by those we had eliminated earlier, and others of
their ilk might well follow their pattern. Returning along
my way, roughly, I was gladdened to find that not a village showed any sign of life. All had heeded my warning,
though in older and more common times it had been hard,
indeed all but impossible at times, to get any new notion
through their hard, shrewd heads. The year of the Warlock's reign had made changes, indeed, if it made my
tough hillmen bolt for hiding at the first whisper of warning.

A corax was my informant, at last. As I made my cautious way along the lip of a steep cut, the purple-black
scavenger shrieked its raucous warning from the deeps
below me, flying upward toward me, full of malefactions
for those who had disturbed its feeding among the
thickets beside the burn. I sank to stillness, that it might

not, in turn, warn those I sought that I was about. But it missed seeing me and flew into the wood past the ridge, still squawking; and then the deeps were broken by a faint clank as a scabbard touched another bit of gear.

As I moved down into the ravine, I could smell the tang of smoke, hanging low to the ground. On the steep slope where I now traveled, the thick overhang of branches and the pitch of the angle had either held off or slid downhill most of the snow, and I was able to slip along quietly as a ghost on the mat of damp fir needles underfoot. So I lay on my belly and crawled the last few furlongs, which enabled me to spot and evade the pickets that had been posted about the camp.

The slavers had a penchant for camping under the protecting wall of a sheer embankment. This was much of a kind with that other camp, saving only the lack of prisoners. They had a much larger fire, too, and a slain hornbeast roasted, whole, above it on a spit. But, for all their comfort, they were alert and armed, and not one had slipped off his mail shirt or put by his blade. But I had not intended attacking them, now, even though the red and berserk rage boiled within me fit to burst my seams.

I had no doubt that they had been sent to clear the high villages and, finding them empty and with no trace of victims to haul back to their commanders, were even now preparing to retrace their steps to rejoin whatever larger group they had been detailed from. I proposed to move with them, so I found a spot that was shielded by undergrowth from any upslope or below and burrowed into it, well within earshot of the group about the fire.

It was as well, for these men were Krel—or at least their common tongue was Krellar. Though much of their private conversation was only a mutter, I could hear well when they talked across the circle. And they spoke bitterly of their commander, one Zorek, and even more bitterly of their present project.

"This be no work for *men*," a bearded youth said crisply, as he cut a strip from the roasting haunch and settled beside an older man. "I made one with Zorek for the pay, yes, for his mercenaries are known and feared from the Harral to the Shern, and he commands top wage for himself and his men. But never did I think to be sent into frozen wastes to make slaves of free folk like my own. Glad I am that those blundering beasts from Rikkar frightened all the villagers away. It would sit sour on my belly to do the thing we were hired to do. A plague on warlocks, say I, with no exceptions!"

His companion grunted with laughter. "Few have your nice ways, Kerrel. But I must admit that none of us are taken with the task, or with the taskmaster. A rare hand at bargaining he is, too. Even Zorek, blast his tough old liver, was unpleased with the bargain he had to strike, at the last. I heard him tell Wurd that had we not made so long a trek to come here, and it a dead loss to go back empty-handed, he would have walked away from the whole agreement and gone another way. That wizard turned us all cold in our guts, when we went with Zorek to make the bargain. Cold as a frog's toenails, he seems, with a look in his eye that would make you padlock your treasure vault and guard your wife."

"You could have voted on it!" exclaimed the younger, carefully wiping the grease from his beard with a handful of snow. "The Old Guard has the right. Why did you not take Zorek aside and cast the lots?"

"We asked ourselves that, when all was sealed and irretrievable," the older man answered. "I think, and not alone, mind you, that we were enspelled, even Zorek, for all his thunder-stone charm. Our wits were far a'wandering, while that squeamy serpent charmed us to his will."

I, in my hidden nook, nodded agreement. Some such I suspected had been the reason my father made his mad wager, drank that undoubtedly tainted wine, and lost the kingdom that our forebears had carven from wilderness and haunted grasslands. That some such deceit had been used to warp honest mercenaries into going slaving would explain much. And even the Rikkar, wild though their reputations were, must have been ensnared in the same way. Murderers and thieves though they no doubt were, I had never heard that they went hunting for men. Only the Krel supplied the wants of those barbarians across the Harral who yoked their fellows into servitude.

I was comforted, somewhat, by the thought that I was not committed to follow a band of beasts back to their source. Mercenaries I knew well, having been one myself in those far-off days when I went from Lantir, after bitter words with my father, and threw all my seventeen years of energy and unwisdom into learning the arts of war. Kerrel and his companion and the grizzled old stump of a sergeant I had known behind many faces, then. The scars those years had laid on my hide were many, but they did not match the gravings of experience and memory they etched into my heart. The like of Zorek, I had no doubt, had also commanded me, more than once.

With no prisoners, and no prospect of any, my quarry set their night watch and settled for the night. As good soldiers should, they laid their weapons beside them under their blankets, and they left their coverings loose, that no night attack might find them bound and helpless in their own bedrolls. Smiling, I rolled myself tightly into my furs and set myself to sleep lightly but well. I could see no likelihood of anyone's attacking a snow-covered bush between midnight and dawn, and I needed the rest.

The next two days were wearying to one of my temperament. Silent stalking with the prospect of immediate game for the table is one thing. The same thing with no aim but following is less interesting. So, once I had determined their firm direction, I cut around my guides and went with more speed. That night, I sat before a fire of my own, thawing out my frosted bones and cooking, for once, some crisply sizzling meat of my own. Then I sat and gazed into the fire, seeking for Varil.

She came glimmering into life, there among the embers, and I smiled to see her. Before she could speak, I said to her, "Varil, my wench, I am minded to wed and become a family man. What think you of it?"

"And who would you wed, Karas?" she asked innocently. "What proper maid, suitable to your station and acceptable to the nobles of Lantir, would link her life with yours in your present dilemma?"

I grunted. "Little did I grieve to see the kingdom wrested from my father's hands, simply on account of you, my love. And now, if I retrieve it through my own efforts, I will be suited to make my own rules of succession. Any noble families who object to my wedding with the loveliest sorceress between the Harral and the Shern may keep their lips tight or find another ruler who will let them dictate his life."

She laughed with pleasure, there in the deeps of the coals, but her face grew serious as she said, "You give me hope, Karas, and I thank you for it. But there is many a mile between wishing and having. And something new stirs in the wind. Have you felt the prod of the Warlock's needle in the past days?"

I thought back and found with astonishment that I had not. Indeed, I had been so busy with my tasks that I had forgotten about that pain beneath the ribs that had been with me so constantly before. "No," I told her. "For days I've not thought of it. Does the attention of the Warlock wander?"

"Your father has come down from the heights where he hid with old Grom. I have watched him with a farseeing eye, and he wavers as he comes, but he moves steadily, for all that. Word came to him, even there, of the harassment of his people, and he brings his aching bones down to do battle for them, futile though it may be. From his direction, I think that he intends to do battle directly with the Warlock. And that wizard thinks the same, for he has turned all his mind from you and the people of the hills, the plain, and of Antri."

"Then I must turn from my path and go to him!" I breathed. "He is too frail, by your own word, to be left alone in this untoward cold."

"Grom is with him," she answered calmly. "You may not think that one who walks beneath such weight of years as he can be of great help, but Grom is more than any of you. He cannot read the holy writings, true, but he has great native wit, honed to sharpness by years of use and problem solving. He has never let his fear sway him from his own path, no matter if both swords and sorceries stood in his way. Had his folk, in the oldest of days, not shunned cities and the company of men, he might well have sat upon the throne, and the name of our nation might be Growemme, instead of Lantirion. Give no part of your strength over to concern for your father. He is in good hands."

"Yet, I fear for him," I said. "Much though we have

quarreled in our lives, still we have much affection between us."

"It may ease you even more to know that one is coming, even through the snows that cloak the lands between these mountains and the Bay of Antri, to stand beside your father. Her name is Mowen, and she is a priestess sent by Him Who Calls Upon the Name." Varil cupped her hands beneath her chin and nodded twice, in the gesture of reverence, and I did the same.

"Then even the gods, busy with their strange games, have set their eyes upon Lantirion," I mused.

"True," she answered. "And your task is to see to these intruders into the country. Many of them are simple soldiers, but some few are ravening beasts, and all are a terrible danger to your people. They, I truly believe, are the agency whereby the attention of the gods was drawn to this struggle. The gods, I know from my probings into things unseen, pay little heed to the doings of the great and powerful, but the cries of the oppressed and endangered wake them to action."

"Then I will go about my work in confidence," I said. "And you go about yours in the knowledge that if we live I will come to you to ask that you become my wife, the mother of the heirs of Lantirion."

She laughed. "Karas, you are sometimes so very stuffy. It may be that I will do as you wish. Or it may not. I have my own work to do, in the short span of my life, and I must think long before I assume such a time-consuming thing as being a princess. Let us go on with our tasks, and let it be as the gods will it, in the end."

She winked out, leaving me cold and disconsolate in the night and the snow. Only the thought of winning again to that shabby hut in the western forests had comforted me in my going. To lack that one warm surety was to lack a deep lying purpose in all that I did.

But I rose before first light and went on, nevertheless. Let my fate be what it would, my family had taken upon themselves the responsibility for the well-being of Lantirion when they gave it their name and the rulership of their blood, and I was bound by older bonds than any I had made in my thirty years of life.

CHAPTER 7

Zorek had made his central encampment along the edge of the Threll, a stream that began as a rill high in the mountains and ended as one of the major tributaries of the Shern. As it left the foothills, it had cut a wide valley into the rich soil, and ages upon ages had filled that vale with huge trees and small meadows thick-grown with grass and herbs. It was a wise commander's choice, covered over as the land was, now, with the snows of this uncommonly cold winter. There was ample wood for fires, shelter in the fir forest for horses, and forage, though winter-killed and with depleted strength in it, under the snow, which the wise beasts pawed aside to find the gray-tan grasses.

I applauded his shrewdness, even as I raged at his purpose in being on the ground of Lantirion. So many and alert were his pickets that I was forced to keep my distance. Still, I was able to see, from the top branch of a giant tree, well enough to estimate his numbers and to determine the layout of his camp. And I saw to my fury that he held some few prisoners.

They were not hillfolk, I made certain from the bright colors of their tattered garments. Besides, I knew from my own investigations that all the hill villages were now in safety. Still, these were my people, too, though I had never been close to those of the plain as I had been to the folk of Antri and the hills.

They were contained in a rough stockade built of fir saplings, and I was relieved to see that rude huts had been thrown up for their shelter, and good fires blazed at three points in their enclosure. I judged from that that fair amounts of food had been provided for them. Zorek had a goodly grasp of the economics of slaving—a dead or emaciated and sickly slave is far less profitable than a strong and hardy one. And if his bargain had been so little to his liking, he was probably seeing to it that the profits to be made would be as large as possible.

Having found what I sought, I drew back into the forested hills and found a sheltered spot that would conceal me from patrols, as well as from that group that would be coming in soon from the direction I had come from. With a large army to bar my way, I must have time to consider how to free my people, before I took steps to drive that force from my lands.

I dared not risk a fire, but I closed my eyes and thought of Valir with all my strength. Behind my eyelids, her dim face took form, and I asked, "Have you seen my father, love?"

She nodded. "He is still upon the steeps of the mountains. He comes slowly, because the snows have made the ways impassable to any but the madly determined. Grom knows ways that others have forgotten—or never knew— for traversing deep snows, so the two of them move steadily. But it will be many days before they win down to the level of the Warlock's keep. Even then, he will be a great distance from that perilous place, and the two of them will be forced to cover miles and miles of difficult country before drawing near to it."

"Then I may sleep without worry," I said. "I am contriving a game that my enemies may find it disconcerting to play, but it will require much of my energies. Fare you well, my Lady."

I lay back in the folds of my cloak, but her image did not fade. "Sleep deeply, Heir of Lantir," she said, gently. "I will watch for you, so that you need set no inner guard. Have no fear, for if any approach too closely, I will wake you."

So I slept the night away in one black velvet drift, relaxed to the bone, and warm, despite the biting cold that lay over the lands. The presence of Valir's conscious thought banished any tension that might have marred my rest, and I woke to her command in the first light of dawn.

"Karas!" she called, and I sat up instantly. "There are those upon the plain beyond Threllside who come with death in their eyes and hands and hearts. Zorek holds their kin, and they come to die with them, knowing that the body of men who guard will be far more than they can hope to overthrow."

"The plains people were ever overbold," I said. "I will take thought for them immediately. And my thanks to you, Varil, mistress of many arts, for your care through the night."

She smiled and was gone, and I chewed a bit of cold meat, washed it down with wine from Shal's modest store, and took thought. If the people were just beyond the Threll, it would be wise for them to delay their attack until night came again . . . if, indeed, they could conceal their presence from Zorek's busy patrols. I must go to them at once, dangerous though it might be to my plans to chance being detected. And I must go now, before full day. I gathered up my pack, strapped it on, and slipped through the forest like the cat hunters of the heights.

I did not try to go the easy way, following the course of Threll. Instead, I cut directly over the tops of the intervening hills. I made no attempt to cover my tracks, for the wood was crisscrossed with the trails of patrols and of single scouts, coming and going about the business of Zorek. This made my going swift, indeed, for Shal and I had cut our teeth upon snow-covered hills much steeper than these by Threllside.

More than once, I was forced from my purposes to hide from those who walked abroad, guarding these approaches to Zorek's camp. Once, I came face to face with a great bear of a man. He was hung about with furs until he seemed, in truth, some human incarnation of a beast, but his blade was swift enough, for all that. Not to mention his eyes, that took me in and decided at a glance that, whatever I might be, I was none of Zorek's.

Pale eyes glinted at me over the edge of his embossed shield, and the sword in his hand was hilted with gemmed gold, so I knew that this one must stand high in the army below. Perhaps he was an officer of the Old Guard that Kerrel had mentioned, all those nights ago. He moved, however, with the speed and precision of a twenty-year-old, and I sidestepped his rush, intending to trip him as he passed and to cut his throat before he could rise.

He was surefooted as a dancer. He leaped my thrusting foot, whirled in midair, and came down a short arm's length away. I parried his strokes easily enough, but their force rang against my star-steel blade like the hammer of a smith upon an anvil. My fingers numbed with the vibration, and I knew that, powerful though I had ever been, I had met my match in this northerner.

I gave ground, testing out his techniques. He was wary as a cat, and those terrible strokes kept clanging with rhythmic precision upon my weaving blade. Then I girded up my loins for desperate effort, remembering what it would mean to my people below if I died here in the snow at the hands of such a warrior.

Keeping him occupied with my blade, I reached out with my inner ability and caught up a log of wood that lay a few paces away. It came whirling through the air, straight at his head . . . but I could not strike down such a magnificent fighter with such wizardlike tactics. I let the log drop beside him, and he leaped backward, expecting attack from others at his back. He looked at the log, examined the snow, keeping a wary eye on me all the while. No tracks save our own stained the winter cloak of snow.

"Did you do that?" he grunted in heavily accented Krellar, and I nodded, lifting the log and setting it back in the spot from which I had brought it. Then I waited, a plan forming in my mind while he pondered.

"Who?" he asked, at last, shrugging his furs into place and lowering his blade.

"Karas Lantir, Heir of Lantirion, until the Warlock stole the kingdom from my sire," I answered. "Your people are here, I'd wager, because *my* people resisted my banning and would not claim the bounty upon my head."

He understood Krellar only slowly, but his wits, once the words were interiorly translated, caught the meaning quickly. There was no trace of doubt in his eyes, when he looked at me. Only, and it warmed me to see it, a grudging respect.

"Harl Indvor," he said, striking his massive chest with his shield. "No slaver, though caught in the toils of slaving, now. Zorek, curse his liver, was bemused by yon Warlock, also. No man of his, save only the Rikkar (curse them, too), is willingly here. And I am—or was, until only now—deserting. Death is the penalty, should I be taken, but my heart will die, if I go on with this *yin-faerhling* bargain Zorek made."

"Does any know you have left them?" I asked.

"I am on scout," he answered. "There is not one in that camp of my blood, only one of the folk who gave me lifeplace, Wurd—snakespawn!" he hissed. "Not one of the others is of any kin-spirit with me. So I told no one of my plan."

I gestured toward a thicket on the higher slope of the hill where we had fought. "Come with me, Harl Indvor, if you will. I have a word I would say to you, and if you agree, it may be that both of us will prosper . . . or die."

He nodded, and we moved together into concealment and sank on our haunches, both for shelter and for concealment. Then I said, "My people are captive in that camp down there. Others of my folk will try to free them, soon or late. I must aid both, but it is difficult even for me" (here I embellished the truth rather much) "to be in two places at one time. I need one whom I can trust to remain in that place, ready to aid the captives when attack comes from without.

"It will be a fearfully dangerous task for that one. He must be trusted by Zorek . . . trusted enough to guard the captives. He must be close-mouthed as the dead. And he must be one of wit enough to let my people know that he is there to aid them, without also revealing himself to the Krel . . . or the Rikkar."

"It would be a task for a hero—a very Gunda-Hralo," said Harl, slowly. "Much virtue would the good Gaerl find in one who came to him in the upper world on the wings of such a deed. But what if that one lived on? Where would he find a place in this world that judges a mercenary solely by the faith he keeps with his leaders?"

I smiled (internally only) and answered, "If such a one

lived, and I succeed in the task I have set myself, that one would have the gratitude of a king, with the just reward that gratitude would bestow. A place at court, or a bit of land, or a ship in which to go venturing, or all three. No man has ever accused Lantir of tight-fistedness."

Harl looked me long in the eye. "There are men," he said at last, "who mistrust every word spoken in their ears, men who are unable and unwilling to judge the speaker, weighing him in the balance of their own experience and wisdom. Not so am I. Pride have I in judging men truly, and I know you for a prince and a teller of truth; as well as a warrior skilled beyond any I have met before. I will go back. I will guard your captive people and set them free at the time that will come. And my reward will be in your hands . . . if Gaerl will that both of us live to reckon it."

I reached for his hand, and we clenched grips about wrists in the sign of bonding. Then the huge man stood amid the bushes and tested his stance.

"Many a stroke you gave me that will make me walk lame for a time," he said. "That will be reason enough for Zorek to set me guarding instead of scouting. Wish me well, Karas Lantir. And Gaerl go with you."

Without another word, he turned and moved away through the trees, and I watched him out of sight before leaving the covert in the opposite direction. And now I moved with more caution, for if Zorek had any other like to Harl, I did not want to meet him this day . . . or ever. Like Harl, I, also, had reason to limp, and I took care that no blood might fall in my track to make me an easy quarry.

When I reached the crest of the last of the hills, I could see far out over the plains. The expanse of snow seemed unbroken. Not a dot of black man-shape, not a point of color indicated that man had ever walked there. But I knew that Varil always saw truly, and I set myself to divine the place where my people waited, as well as the best way to come there without betraying my presence, or theirs.

Long I lay in the scanty forest that dwindled to nothing on the western slope of this final hill, watching for Zorek's lookouts. But I saw none, and I realized at last that I had found the chink in that canny man's armor. He discounted the plains people, a serious error on his part. He thought those who remained to be quivering sheep, awaiting his herding.

The thought of sheep struck a light in my mind. Though the plains seemed even as a table, still they were not, for they rolled in gentle undulations that ran north and south, paralleling the two mountain chains that bracketed the flatlands. And in the lowest troughs of those undulations, the plainsfolk made their sheep herds' wintering shelters, stocked with long windrows of hay, and covered over with branches gathered from the adjacent forests. When the snow came, it smoothed whitely over all, sheltering the sheep with a frozen roof. There, I felt sure, were my people, safely hidden with their own sheep to keep them warm, waiting for darkness to fall.

That internal map that my tutors had written onto my mind held the location of very sheep shelter in all the plains. The one nearest this part of the Threll lay only two or three hours' trek to westward, even in such deep snow. I need only set myself in line between that shelter and Zorek's camp, and they would find me, eliminating the need for moving outward across that revealing white coverlet.

CHAPTER 8

Night came at last. It had been a long afternoon, cramped into the skimpy shelter of a patch of briers whose lack of density made it dangerous to move, lest I catch the eye of some unseen watcher. Still, darkness fell over the plains, leaving them as black and featureless as a well in a cave. I knew that now my people were moving. I felt certain that Zorek would keep no watch in this direction at night, for it would be useless for seeing anything except a procession bearing torches. So I waited with shortening patience for the first hint of movement.

Sound carries with terrible clarity across snow, but I heard nothing until they were almost upon me. Then it was only the faint crunch of a foot sinking into the snow that alerted me. I stood upright, leaving my thorny haven with relief.

"Ssssssss!" I hissed into the blackness.

There was total silence, and I knew that every man and woman had frozen where he stood, listening. I set my voice to that space that falls between whisper and voice and said, "Karas Lantir stands with you. A friend guards our people. There is hope. Let us go!"

One multitudinous sigh wafted across the chill air, and I knew that they had heard. Then we moved swiftly and silently toward Zorek's camp, and well before midnight we reached it.

The clouds of the past days had fled eastward at twilight, and a sky of blazing stars gave us a bit of light to steer by. Neither moon was up, which was as well, for so much brightness can betray a secret attack. In that tenuous almost-seeing, we divided our force, which numbered some thirty, and sent two tens to cover the ways upstream and down.

When they had time to position themselves, I stood on the ridge that marked the bank of the Threll at its highest point and gave a great shout. Shouts answered me from the other parties, and all of us fell onto the startled Krel with steel and fury. The red rage that I had suppressed for so long seized me in its grip, and I waded through ranks of mailed men as if they were rows of grain or cattle. Their blades ripped my flesh in many places and rang from my metal helm like a carillon of bells, but I felt neither pain nor fear. The heads I mowed from their native shoulders, the arms and hands I lopped off made a trail, I was told later, by which my small army followed me into the melee.

But I was past knowing or caring. I was a machine of war, nothing else, and my only memories from that battle are of thrusts and parries, of pain-mad faces, shocked into death. I moved, I remember, through a troop of Rikkar. My sole thought was to kill every one of them before moving on, but surely that would have been impossible. They were all dead behind me, but I feel certain that a body of my own folk must have scythed through them with me. Only modesty would make them deny it, afterward.

I only came to myself when I reached the stockade. Sounds of battle came from within, and I hacked loose a great section of the lattice wall, letting it tumble before leaping over it. Inside, I could see that Harl had backed the other guards into a corner, while my people unshackled themselves and caught up lengths of chain to use as weapons.

"Lantir!" I cried, and they turned toward me. I gestured toward those Harl Indvor was battling. "Aid him, for he is our friend!" I shouted, and a handful hurried to assist the great northerner. They caught up parts of the shattered wall, long rods of tough wood, and used them to crown their erstwhile guards, while Harl neatly skewered one and whirled to gut his fellow. By then, the other six were laid low, and Harl turned to join me.

"Out and up!" I shouted, pointing toward the hills with my swordblade. "Those who are hurt or ill or weak go first, with the upstream ten! Harl, we will hold the rear while they run clear."

My tiny army struggled its way to my side, and I found that with Harl and some score of the ex-captives who were still fit enough to fight, we had a tough, though small, wedge of flesh and steel to drive into any of Zorek's men who grew too brave in their pursuit. With pride, I saw the freed prisoners catch up their young, their wounded, and their sick and make for the forest with speed that would have done credit to fresh troops.

When they were well clear, those who had guarded their flight came back into the fray, moving forward to give our surviving fighters a chance to catch their breath.

The pride of Zorek lay along the edge of the Threll, more than a hundred picked and ready troops . . . a banquet for the eagles. Those who yet held weapons were wary men, their education well begun in the folly of discounting any of Lantirion, old or young, man or woman, captive or free. And their very numbers hampered them, for we backed away, a hedgehog bristling with sharp blades, and only a few could attack us at once. We left none, wounded or dead, for the imaginations of the Rikkar who still lived to play with. While this might have seemed foolish, those who could walk bore those who could not, and no man able to fight needed to carry his wounded comrade.

When we reached the snowy slopes, we broke formation and fled into the deep forest, counting on our desperation to help us outdistance our pursuers. And there is an art to running uphill in deep snow that few soldiers learn. We could hear them slipping and slithering and tumbling downhill in cursing heaps, but we ran on. And soon there was no sound behind us but the distant shouts and buglings and cries of pain.

When the need for great speed lessened, we cast about for the trail of those who had gone before us. It was not hard to find, for so many feet trample the snow to slush. I looked at that clear sky beyond the fir tips and wished for more snow, but the stars stared coldly down, and no cloud answered my prayer. So I turned to Harl, who had stayed doggedly by my side, and said, "Friend Harl, what say you to sending all these ahead, while we contrive to hide their trail?"

He grinned, his white teeth glinting in the starlight. "You ask a master, Prince. We of the north have tricks that southrons little dream of. Send them on . . . they well deserve a bit of good luck. I have seen seasoned troops do less well on field of battle than these. You do well, Lantir, to care so for such folk."

So we sent our companions forward, and the marks of many dragging feet, more than one ooze of blood shone dark on the starlit snow. Harl directed them to catch up to the first group and hold together, resting, until we followed. Then he looked upward.

"Good trees here, Prince," he said. "Very thick, very tall and slim. Much snow rests in their tops."

I raised my head again and saw how the light snow clung in frosted riffles upon the needled branches overhead. Harl seized a bole in his bearlike arms and heaved until the whole tree shook, and a storm of snow whirled down about our ears. I laughed aloud and caught a tree trunk in my own embrace. I shook it, and a whole shelf of white stuff slipped off and fell about me.

We made our own snowstorm, Harl and I, moving along the track, then turning to shake down more over the entire trail. The result was uneven, lumpy, unnatural-looking to the trained eye. But it was night, and we were sure that Zorek, stinging under his surprise and defeat, would not wait for day to send his men on our trail. Their eyes were not those of hillmen, and few, Harl said, were even countrymen, much less foresters. By the time they had scrambled and trampled over the hillsides, even Harl himself would be hard put to find where we had walked.

It was not a quick task, and before we were done we could hear the calls of those who had come to the end of the tracks that they had followed. But they were far away, and there had been no way, amid the thick woods, for them to determine the general direction of our trail. They cast about, and I could not fault their training. But training will not substitute for expertise, and we reached our waiting friends after leaving our pursuers far out of earshot.

The night was paling to dawn, and to my delight I saw an edging of cloud catching the first pink rays of the rising sun. The Warlock, I knew in my bones, had sent this foul winter as punishment to his unruly country. But if he again sent snow, it would work against him. What we most needed was a blizzard to hide our tracks.

We now had with us some fifteen of our original thirty rescuers, together with over a hundred of their freed kindred. We had, I estimated, some seventy or eighty dead, most of those from the stockade, who had been dead or dying when they were taken away from the camp. Our wounded were mostly ambulatory. Those dead we had been forced to leave in the first press of battle we sorely lamented, but such had been the circumstances that we could have done nothing else but let them lie where they fell.

We knew that we must dispose of the dead, then find refuge for the living. I longed for Shal or Grem, knowing that either of them would know of some secure place to put the bodies, where they would not be found by enemies or devoured by beasts. The plainsfolk used the forests, at intervals, but they were not really familiar with the hills. As I mulled over the problem, one of my uphill pickets whistled the call of a disturbed snowbird.

In a bit, I looked up and saw Shal moving toward me, accompanied by Harl. I shot from my seat on a cold, damp stump and threw my arms about him.

"The gods sent you, Brother!" I said. "We need your knowledge."

He grinned in the morning light, but I could see lines on his face that had not been there when we met before. "I see a part of your trouble," he answered. "But if your companions can bear their dear burdens yet a while, I know of a spot where they can rest until there is time and opportunity to sing the rituals over them."

I looked over the exhausted group that huddled together for warmth in the shelter of the trees. To any eye but mine, they might have seemed at the end of their resources, unable to go farther themselves, far less to carry

their dead with them. But I now knew these people better
than I ever had before.

"They will carry them to the Warlock's door, if it be
necessary," I said, and Shal looked at me with an odd
quirk to his quizzical mouth.

But Harl, on my other side, said in his awkward
Krellar, "So will they, Hillman. These folk are not as
others I have seen in the years I warred behind Zorek.
Their spirits burn inside their flesh, and they wear their
pain and their weariness as one would wear a tattered
cloak, with indifference. See you that woman?" and he
pointed toward a middle-aged woman who sheltered beneath her torn robe a nest of children.

"I watched her, there in the stockade. When the shout
came for the attack, she moved like a flash of light, rank-
ing the young ones in order, the older to carry the
youngest, the middle to aid those smaller. A soul like a
general, she has. She killed with her bare hands a guard
who came with his sword bared to scatter her charges.

"She has run all night, carrying more than one small
one, I'd warrant. Now she warms them with her body,
having no other source of heat. She has fed them fir tips.
She has melted snow in her hands for them to drink.
None of those little ones are hers . . . her child died the
day before yesterday, she told me as I guarded them.

"Truly, a people so nurtured can carry burdens that
others might faint to think on." He fell silent, and we two
others said no word.

We passed the day in quiet . . . and cold. No fire could
be built, for the smoke would surely have betrayed us to
our enemies. Those of us who possessed warm garments
shared them out among the very young and the very ill,
whom Shal had packed together in groups of twelve or so

beneath the low-sweeping branches of some of the young
firs. With the snow swept from the needled floor into
packed bastions, the warmth of their own bodies aided
them, under the blanket of boughs we covered them with.

They made no complaint, though to sickness and
wounds was added frostbite. But when the day waned,
and we made ready to travel again, they were ready to
move, for a night of sleep, here in the cold wood, meant
that many would never waken. We helped them struggle
to their feet, and those who could stand grimly set one
foot before the other. The dead—and those who were
soon to be so—we carried, taking turns, those of us who
were whole, at bearing them away up the slopes toward
the mountains.

For now we made no casts back and forward to find villages. We knew that no village was now tenanted, and that
any buildings in which we sought to shelter would prove
to be traps, should Zorek's men come that way. Now we
made as straight a line as could be for the nearest mountains that brooded invisibly to the east. Cloud-Cap hung
close by, though the hills and the forests closed away any
glimpse of it. We slogged desperately through the snow,
guided by the glimmer of snowlight and the unerring instinct of Shal and Grem, who had come with his friend.

It was a terrible journey. Many whom we carried died
in our arms as we went. The dead stiffened into chill stat-
ues, most difficult to bear with any ease. But we left none
to mark our trail, though we knew that we could be followed with ease by a half-grown child. Still, there was no
time for covering our tracks. Only arrival at our destina-
tion must be allowed to slow us, now, for we knew that if
we halted again it might well be never to rise again.

Had it been a great distance, we would have perished
there in the snowy forests, for our bodies had been tried
far past anything the human frame was meant to endure.

But with another dawn, we faced the sheer cliff that marked the knee of Cloud-Cap, and Shal and Grem gave over their burdens to others and hurried away to a secret store of gear the hillfolk kept nearby for climbing that cliff. When the sun cast the mountain's bulk as a jagged black shape against the rosy east, they were aloft, rigging slings for moving the helpless upward.

I had never been a parent. Perhaps a father looks with equal pride on the strivings of his children to that pride with which I saw my battered, tattered people attack that terrible climb. A prince, perhaps, is parent to all his folk. I all but wept, as I saw withered graybeards set their bloodied feet and frozen hands on the slight holds the face provided and move upward, shepherding before them a child or a pregnant girl, or a warrior so wounded that he was not sure in his grip or his wits. All who could, climbed. Those who were unconscious or totally disabled, they alone rode up in the slings.

It was a long task, but we accomplished it with fewer casualties than I would have dared to hope for, at its beginning. Those who fell were also brought up, at the last, and their honoring was no less than that for those dead in battle. When the sun shone full onto the cliff, beginning its western descent, we stood, all who lived, on the lofty ledge that topped the front of Cloud-Cap and saw tiny figures in the now-distant forests that were the troops of Zorek.

Among the tumbled boulders that edged the shelf, we laid our dead, covering them with cairns, safe from beast or bird. Then we climbed again, before limbs could stiffen to uselessness. Night found us going up and up, following the chimneys and crannies that led upward to the old fortress that had sat upon the crest of Cloud-Cap since the earliest days, long before our folk had come to live in Lantirion.

We came to those grim ruins in the first light of another dawn, with snowflakes just beginning to fall about our numb shoulders. They bulked in tapered squares, outwall, tower, and inner keep, solid as the very buildings of Antri, though older than memory itself. And, though hillmen dreaded them and shunned them when they could, the old keep was stocked for emergency uses with firewood. Many a climber after the goats of the mountains had survived a blizzard here, when otherwise he would have died. And each had carefully replenished the store of wood, hoisting it painfully all that dizzy way up the height.

So we were able to build fires in the ancient guardroom, where the thickness of walls silenced the wind howl that now began to rage across the stony height. Goatskins had been rough cured and left for future use, and they were of more comfort to us than downy beds and woolen coverlets had ever seemed. We were able to warm our hurt and our sick. The great pot that hung over the larger of the two fireplaces was filled with snow, and we were able to wet our leathery tongues, cut and sore from eating snow.

When we had everyone as comfortable as we could manage, we fell into sleep. Even the urgings of our long-empty stomachs could not disturb our rest, and we slept the day away and part of another night. And when Shal and Grem stood beside me again, in the light of another day, we could see that the new snow had again covered our track. It would be a while before Zorek would again pick it up, though we knew that he would persist until he did.

"We must find food," said Shal, on my left, and I nodded.

CHAPTER 9

We left our companions asleep, with fresh fires roaring in the fireplaces. With ropes and knives and a pair of ancient lances that had hung upon the wall, we went up yet again, searching for the goats that sheltered in unexpected notches of steaming springs and lasting grass, even here on the very roof of Lantirion. And we returned to our people with three of them.

Harl had slept long and deeply, and when we brought in our prey he took upon himself the task of skinning and readying them for cooking. So the folk woke to the smell of broth steaming in the great pot, and of haunches sputtering over the coals. Color returned to wan cheeks, and everyone who could rose to take his turn dipping from the pot with the scanty utensils in the keep.

After close examination of the very weak, I concluded that those who were like to die had already gone from us. These would recover, in time, given rest and good food. And time we must give them.

Calling Harl, Shal, and Grem, I went again to the crumbled portal that looked out over the hills below. It was again night, and we could see the points that marked Zorek's campfires. They were distant . . . but not distant enough. They were free to move about the lands below, to the danger of all my hidden ones there. They were free, should the notion take them, to turn toward Antri, and the folk of Antri were not so tough, so bold, or so knowing as these less civilized people.

"We must destroy Zorek's army," I said.

The three looked at me in the starlight, as if to judge my sanity.

"We are pent up on this mountain," I said. "Zorek walks freely below. But we are at the end of a climb, taxing even for hale warriors fresh from food and rest. And our pursuers will be burdened with mail and weapons. Think on it . . . we are armed with weapons enough to bury Antri, if we should be so minded and could heave them so far." I looked about at the chaos of boulders that had crumbled from the bluff that backed the fortress and at the stubby tooth of rock that jutted upward almost at the edge of the drop.

"The ledge is a first line of defense. Think of the rubble there. There are boulders large enough to carry away this fortress, if they could be set rolling. And our own dead would glory to be hurled down upon their murderers in defense of their own folk."

They said nothing, for then, but I could see their thoughtful faces, and I was satisfied to let them think the thing through for themselves. In silence, we turned back into the old citadel, taking up our duties of caring for those unable to care for themselves. But there was, in truth, little for us to do. The fitter among them had begun to organize themselves into duty details, and Renath, the woman Harl had so admired, was assigning tasks and seeing that all was done that need be.

For three days we rested on Cloud-Cap, hunting goats in the late afternoon when they moved to their nightly sheltering spots. Shal disappeared for a half-day and reappeared laden with roots and shoots and twigs that Renath fell upon with cries of delight. Added to the soup made from the goat bones and scrap meats, they strengthened the ill visibly. On the third day all but a handful of our complement were able to walk about, helping where they could.

Then I judged it time to take up the grave matter of Zorek's army. Gathering all together before the roaring fires (stoking them was the children's task, but providing the fuel occupied many men's time and much effort), I looked into their faces. There were pale faces, scarred ones, sorrowful ones, but no frightened ones, even among the small ones.

With a lifting heart, I waved them to silence and said, "We have come out of dreadful danger into safety, unlikely though that looked a few days ago. But the men who took you and yours captive are still there in the foothills, searching for us. Many of our fellow countrymen are hidden, hillfolk who have their secret warrens for refuge. Zorek may well find many of them, if he is left to roam at will over our lands. Or he may turn against Antri, which will leave both plains and hill people without a market for their hides and meat and herbs, and without a source of any of the things that make your rough lives easier.

"I have a mad plan . . . the plan of desperate people taking more desperate measures. I want to taunt Zorek from this height, draw him into attack upon us. He will expect a battered lot of slaves to be his only resistance. But, even weak and wounded as we have been, I believe that we are able to destroy the invaders of our lands, even to the last man of them. What say you?"

There was a long silence. I could see the elders thinking deeply, the younger ones catching fire with the boldness of the idea. Renath answered me first, a wriggling child on her knee making her words seem more incongruous.

"Bold measures are best," she said in her thin voice.

"He Who Calls Upon the Name, blessed be his spirit, when he last came into the plain, spoke to us of the folly of mistaking weakness for piety. Be bold in your lives, he told us. Let no man set his foot upon your neck. So I say yes. Let us tempt our tormentor into a foolish action. Then let us destroy him. The gods rejoice at the deaths of wicked men."

Those nearest her nodded agreement. Then old Heor, the patriarch of all the plainsfolk, said, "Though we all die, yet we will triumph. Let it be done!"

It was unanimous, and I looked with pride around the stalwart group, so recently at the end of their strength. Harl smiled at me across the room, and I laughed aloud and said, "If I but had wine, we would drink to the success of our plan. But as we have only snow water and goat broth, let us toast our hopes in these!"

So we quietly enjoyed the evening and went to our rest early. Strange as it may seem, I slept deeply and without untoward dreams, though the face of Varil wove itself into the warp of my fantasies. And the face of my father drifted in and out of my thought, so that I waked with his grizzled countenance freshly before my inner eyes.

We spent the day hard at work, clearing footpaths along the edges of the sheer drops. We pushed the stones so cleared just to the edge, ready to hand, when the time came. And many boulders, far too large to be moved by a man, or even two, we dug under and set levers to, so that when many swung on the protruding shaft the great stones would go bounding away down the cliffs. When darkness again drew in, heralding a clear, cold night, we lit torches that we had prepared, and I set one or two torch-carriers to wander near the edge, now and again, so that their betraying lights could be seen by those encamped in the hills far below us. I knew that Zorek's scouts had eyes that missed little, and I wanted our discovery to seem accidental.

With first light, it became clear that we had succeeded, if only in this first step. From our height, we could see lines of men moving through the forested hills, even under the thick roof of needles, for the weight of snow bore down the branches, leaving spaces where none would ordinarily be. They moved fast, tough and seasoned campaigners that they were, and by mid-morning they had come into the rock-strewn space at the foot of Cloud-Cap.

We lay silent, seemingly unaware of our peril. I wanted all to be busy in that exposed strip of rubble, beneath our unorthodox fire. Harl, beside me, drew in his breath sharply, as those below grew more and more numerous, and I knew that he felt for those who had been his comrades-in-arms. But there was no help for it. They had taken a wage in silver, and they were about to draw another in blood.

Before midday, Zorek's men were beginning the climb. They had fashioned rough scaling ladders from the forest's trees, and they had found among their gear bits of rope, to aid those who climbed the sheerest faces. With their fellows assembled in orderly ranks beneath them, the first group attacked Cloud-Cap's inhospitable breast. Only the rear guard of cooks and hostlers and noncombatants still sheltered in the edge of the wood.

We made ready, all who were fit and hale, on our first line of defense, the ledge that held the bodies of our dead. It was deep enough so that we could crawl along its rear part, invisible to those below. Each of us had an arsenal of stones of throwing size, those of rolling size, and several that were ready to be levered down upon the heads of those below. Above us, the less fit, together with the children, stood ready with even more ammunition to hand than had we.

When the faces of the first climbers appeared at the edge of our shelf, we rose and flung them down, helpless as children. Then we began our deadly game of toss-the-stone, and terrible was the havoc wrought below. But Zorek was no fool. As soon as it was clear to him that there was resistance above, he marshaled his archers, and a shower of death rained down on us.

Though they could not see their targets, still we were so closely crowded on the ledge that any arrow that fell stood a fine chance of finding a victim. Shal dropped beside me, and I drew him quickly into the shelter of a leaning boulder until someone could take him aloft to Renath, who was the healer of our group. I was grazed several times, but my strange luck still held, and no bolt set itself into my flesh.

Our perch became too hot for staying, so I shouted the signal, and we scrambled madly up the crannied declivity to the top, thanking the many gods all the way that it was not a sheer, flat face like that below. Had it been, not one of us would have arrived at the top.

Once up, we ranged ourselves alongside our comrades, and we all set ourselves to hurling death down upon our attackers. We were now too high for any arrow to reach us, and our enemies were ranged below us in ranks too crowded for quick withdrawal. With furious energy, we set the boulders rolling, leaving the climbers to the children to finish off with small stones.

It was terrible to look down. When the boulders hit the ground, they literally splashed gouts of blood in all directions, then rolled on into the wood, leaving scraps where there had been men. After one look, I kept my eyes on my work, and I would not think what it must be like to stand below.

Though it seemed years long, our strangely one-sided battle lasted only a few hours. We were still heaving stones, dripping with sweat, panting like spent runners, when Renath cried out, "Look down, kinsmen! They are no more!"

With dread, I looked, and saw a scene of carnage that surely must be unequaled in all the history of man. Of Zorek's army, only those who had sheltered among the forest trees had been able to retreat beyond the roll of the stones. The warriors grouped below us were dead almost to the last man, though only the gods themselves could have known where the smashed remnants of one ended and those of another began. The climbers had fared better. Even those knocked from the cliff by our hail of rocks were better off than their brothers aground. Many of them lay with broken bones and cracked heads, but alive, while all about them their comrades had been obliterated as by some dreadful act of nature.

Of Zorek there was no trace. Although it might well have been that his were among the terrible fragments at the foot of the cliff, I felt that that canny general would have been well in the rear, observing the attack and ordering any necessary strategies and tactics. So I left the others to go among the dreadful carnage to aid those yet living. I went back into the trees, looking for Zorek.

Even in the forest there were traces of the boulders' work. The trees had suffered a bit, but there were bloody trails to show where they had plowed through cooks at work over their fires, over horses and the men who tended them. There were trails through the snow that showed the flight of those left alive. One such trail was that of many men, and it I followed, feeling that Zorek would try to chivy his survivors, even those not truly warriors, into some sort of order for a retaliation of some kind.

They had gone a long way, very fast, and they had found some pack-horses left alive and used them, as the marked snow plainly showed. But those afoot slowed them a bit, and I felt that Zorek would not expect any to follow him. He would probably stop when he came to the first sheltered spot that was sufficiently distant from the mountain that had been his nemesis. So I did not hurry but set my pace to one that I could hold for hours, stopping only to eat a bit of the roasted goat I had brought with me and to sip from my water bottle.

I smelled them before I heard them, for they were lying quiet in a deep ravine. The acrid scent of fear-sweat is one that is never forgotten, once a man has smelled it. The faint breeze that moved up from the lowlands brought me the effluvium, and I was able to find its source without faltering. The faint horse smell assured me that I was right, and the even fainter smokes of newly kindled dry-wood fires told me that shock was of more danger to most of those below than even the fear of betraying smokes. They were trying to warm the feel of death from their bones.

I walked to the edge of the cut and called down, "Zorek, come forth and meet me, man to man. Karas Lan-tir, who freed the slaves you had captured, who destroyed your army with the aid of a mountain, a fearless people, and the gods, who thirsts for your blood and that of the Warlock who engaged you, calls you forth to make the test of battle."

CHAPTER 10

There was silence, utter and astonished, for a long instant. Then I heard a clamor of voices raised in a senseless babble of languages. A voice rang out, authority in its tones, and the clamor ceased. Then I heard the crunch of footsteps in snow, and there was only one set. Zorek, then, was an honest mercenary, abiding by the rules of combat. It comforted me a bit, standing there alone, to know that.

He was not unmarked. There was a purple-red lump on his cheekbone, just above the latchet of his helm. His old-fashioned cuirass was bent and battered, with brownish splashes of blood in streaks across it. Wherever he had taken up his station, it had been near the scene of action. He held his left arm stiffly, as though it pained him, and I guessed that a medium-sized stone must have hit him squarely on his shoulder.

We were fairly well matched in size, and my long day of stone-heaving and climbing had wearied me more than a little. My small wounds from the arrows of Zorek's archers were still oozing a bit, when I moved too freely, and I felt as if I had been flailed like a bundle of grain. There was no question of my being fit and ready and Zorek's being worn and wounded. We were both exhausted, angry, worried, and sick of death.

I could tell that when I looked into his eyes, even shaded as they were by the lip of his helm. He looked at me with wary speculation, biting his lip as he concentrated on assessing my abilities. I did the same for a space, and we stood there studying one another like two schoolboys, new met at the Master's house. Then I waved toward a small glade, not too far away, and said, "Let us have at it, Zorek, slave trader!"

The epithet stung him. He didn't like the task any more than had the various men of his whom I had overheard, or than Harl, who had left his command. I could tell from his spasmodic blink of pain, and by the slow flush that burned outward from the shelter of his helm.

"Name no names, ex-Prince!" he grunted. "You led your folk so ill that they turned you away, so my employer told me."

"Wherefore their new master sold them to Zorek to resell in the markets of Krel . . . and claimed a hefty percentage of the profits made thereby, I'll wager," I answered. "If you use your head for anything except strategy of war and holding up your helm, perhaps you may come up with some reason why one chosen freely by the people of Lantirion should engage in such unkinglike practice."

He grunted again, without reply, but I thought that his mind was busy, as we walked the short distance to the glade, kicked away the worst depths of snow, and turned to face one another. We saluted gravely, holding our long blades upright before our foreheads and making the Old Sign of Threb, god of battles. Then we stepped back, and he sprang forward immediately from his nether foot, sweeping a vicious cut at my unprotected breast. My protesting legs gave a spring, before my head could tell them to, carrying me aside and under the blow, and I stabbed at his belly, for his cuirass came only just below his waist, and he wore no hampering armor save that.

He, in turn sprang backward, and an unseeable stump

hole hidden by the snow swallowed one foot as he landed, sending him atumble. I stepped back until he could rise, and he touched his hand to his heart in thanks. He was no common mercenary, Zorek. His line was that of a good house . . . perhaps even a onetime kingly one, I guessed. His manner told much about him, to one with eyes to see.

Then we engaged again, exchanging strokes, using every dodge that years of rough-and-tumble, in battles and out, had taught us both. We were matched, reflex for reflex, sinew for sinew. What one thought, the other divined as he put it into practice. Any desperate dodge I attempted, he desperately countered. We fought long, and the day gave way to darkness. But now the smaller moon, that we call Ralias, was rising, and the snow caught its light and made brightness sufficient for seeing.

We had paused for rest, for breathing deeply and quelling our shuddering muscles, when I was made aware of a wrongness within me. Long forgotten, a sharpness made itself known again, digging wickedly beneath my rib cage. The Warlock, all the gods curse his every breath, had thought again of me, lost as I had been to him for so long. And he sought, this time, to kill. I could feel that cruel thorn reaching for my heart, though I lay far in a snowy forest with no wound to show the cause of my agony.

Zorek leaned close above me. I could see a frown on his seamed face, as he studied me in the moonlight. "What ails you, Karas Lantir? Are you so soft that a small tiff like ours lays you low?" he asked in purring Krel. "I had not thought it of you."

The pain almost forestalled my breath, and I gasped for air, past that dire bodkin that seemed to thrust into me. "Warlock," I panted, "Your Warlock keeps my image. He has tortured me thus, many times. This time he means my death. Remember this, Zorek, when again you face

that villain . . . if face him you do." Then I saw the
moon grow smaller and smaller, becoming a mere cinder
that winked out, leaving nothing but blackness. *This is
death*, I thought, as I lost even myself.

From the recollection of Zorek

*We landed at Antri in poor case. The sea passage had been
rough, the food poor, the wine like vinegar. My men were
surly as newly waked bears, and my officers seemed to
have little stomach for our foray into Lantirion.*

*If truth be told, I had my own qualms. Something in
the message that had come to me had rung in my mind
with the false note of a lead coin. Yet the Warlock, lately
King of the land, offered what seemed to be fair terms for
our services. And mercenaries must needs go where they
are needed, else they must take up a new sort of work.*

*As we warped to the wharf, however, I found myself
reexamining the wording of the scroll. Perhaps the quality
of the parchment had impressed me, or the ornate script
in black and red, touched with gold. Something had
diverted my mind from the fact that the exact nature of
our new duties was nowhere outlined. Neither was the
precise amount of our payment.*

*So it was with relief mixed with growing suspicion that
I disembarked from the Sea Slug, saw my men into quarters, and took myself to the Sign of the Scarlet Stag to
wait for the messenger who was supposed to meet me
there.*

*There was much of interest there, indeed, but no mes-
senger, though I waited until the last of the stragglers had
been poured out the wide door, and the innkeeper asked
me politely but firmly to leave so he could lock his estab-
lishment. I followed one other who could still keep his*

feet and found myself in a street into which no light shone from any source.

"Every city in the civilized world sets torches along the ways to light the traveler who is benighted there," I muttered between my teeth. I misdoubted my ability to find my own inn again in this midnight tangle of cobbled streets.

A touch on my elbow sent me into a crouch, my hand filled with the blade that seemed to come at my will. A voice whispered in my ear, "You are summoned to the King. None must know where you go or who you are. Follow my touch, and you will be guided where you wish to go, and then again to your quarters."

One of my calling cannot be cowardly, yet there was something about that whisper that set my neck hair acrawl. It was a cold whisper. The winds that blow over the roof of the world are warmer. And it was cynical. Even whispering, the lungs that sent it forth were polluted with such foulness that their owner could see no virtue in the universe. Or so my bones and my instinct told me—and they have led me, standing, from many a situation that should have left me dead.

"Lead," I breathed, unwilling to sully my words with the ears of this invisible being.

We walked for a long time, and I felt the crowding walls draw away as the streets widened into avenues. Now and again I could hear the tinkle of a fountain, chill though the winter night was, and I wondered by what device those of Lantirion kept them unfrozen. The cobbles underfoot gave way to smoothly dressed stone, but my companion's touch on my arm warned me to step lightly and to keep my heels from ringing against them.

We came at last to a gate. I set my hand stealthily against it, and I found it to be strong metal, disguised by intricate scrollwork. Running my fingers across it at shoulder height, I felt near the center a sigil within an oval frame. It seemed to be a serpent, and I noted it well.

While I was stealthily investigating, my guide was opening a series of locks and latches, by the sounds he made. In a bit, the thing swung open so silently that, my hand being now in my pocket, I would not have known it to be open had he not caught my sleeve and drawn me through it into what must, by the feel of space, have been a large garden.

The sound of another fountain greeted us, and when we followed the curve of the flagged path that swung near it, I could feel warmth steaming from the faintly visible water. That explained the scent of green things, even in the dead of winter, and I nodded to myself at having two anomalies explained with one fact.

We crossed the garden silently, the hothouse atmosphere becoming almost oppressive before we reached a second invisible door. This one led into a gloomy hall that was faintly lighted by a single spherical lamp that hung on a silver chain from the lofty deeps of a domed vault.

I stepped inside, then turned to see my guide enter . . . but he did not. He was gone, as silently as he had come, and I was left alone in that gloomy place to wait upon the convenience of the King.

A step approached the hall through a chamber to my left, and I waited quietly as it came nearer. The emaciated shape that came through the garnet-curtained doorway was tall and straight, but there was an indefinable feel of wrongness to it. The same sort of wrongness that had permeated the letter. The same sort that had enwrapped my guide like an aura. I knew in the way I sometimes have that my guide had been this selfsame man, the Warlock, King of Lantirion.

I made the Mercenaries' Reverence, which is the barest minimum due to a reigning monarch. It was noted, I saw, with some resentment. He, however, said nothing. Neither did I, and we stood for a time, assessing one another.

At last, he raised his right hand and made a gesture with his fingers. The lamp flared into brilliance. The hall leaped into light, and its magnificence became apparent. Rich woods gleamed; velvet hangings framed wondrous tapestries. The statuary depicted people of archaic beauty and costume, yet the faces, through the surface loveliness, were subtly debased. Something about the eyes, the contemptuous curve of the lips, spoke of a folk who knew depravity.

"Excellent work," I said, peering at the nearest, a young girl who seemed to be engaged in fishing with a hand net. Then I looked closer. The bottom of the net was still engaged by the stone, but incised there, very vaguely, was the merest hint of a human face.

"You know something of sculpture?" asked the Warlock, his voice ringing oddly on my eardrums. "I am surprised. I thought that mercenaries thought only of profit and . . . death."

"We were not all always mercenaries," I answered coolly, turning to meet his eyes. "Yet, as that is what we are, we must make our bargain. This must be done in the presence of those who are my oldest and best companions. I cannot, by our compact, contract singly for their services."

His eyes, so deeply sunk beneath his overhanging brows, blazed suddenly bright with anger. I could feel a ripple pass over my face, something like the breath of air that moves over desert at midday. A twinge of unease went through me. This was a madman, and dangerous.

Yet when he spoke it was with control. No trace of his

fury touched his voice. "I did not know this. I must bargain in deepest secrecy, for many conspire against me. How many must attend our . . . arrangement?"

"Eight. The nine of us speak for the entire company. We can meet with you at any time, but the sooner it is planned, the better it will be. Secret work is better done by those whose presence is not obvious, and we occupy the inns all about the quay. So many, even in Antri, must eventually be noticed, if they remain for long."

"Then we will meet tomorrow," he hissed, his eyes once again hooded and his face still. "Just before daybreak, bring your eight and walk toward the north gate. Along the way, you will be joined by one who will bring you to me. I cannot be seen, for I am not, you understand, in the city at all. It must never be known that I came here at this time.

"You will be led back to your inn. Go."

He turned on his heel and stalked away, leaving the hangings to flap dismally behind him. I was glad to see him go, and if a man had not materialized in the darkness behind me and beckoned, I would have gone, alone, to seek my lodgings. The feel of this overwarm place was subtly unclean, as was the air in which the King of Lantirion had stood.

Sunrise found nine of us on the way to the north gate. The way was well marked, so that we had no need to ask directions, and our pace was brisk, in the chill of the frosty morning. Many were about, even so early, so that we were not particularly noticeable, walking by twos and threes with a goodly space between, so as to seem less one group.

The north gate loomed at the end of the way, when we were joined, unobtrusively, by a grubby youth of tender years. Whistling between his teeth, he sauntered along as

*though he had been there all the time. A glance sidewise
from his dark and slanting eyes assured me that this was
the promised guide, and I nodded slightly. We stepped
along together, our teeth still chattering a bit in the frozen
air.*

*The north gate was already open, though there was lit-
tle coming and going between its heavy leaves. Once we
emerged from the shelter of walls and streets, we were
swallowed by a veritable sea of snow. Huge drifts were
piled on either side of the road, which had been packed
down somewhat earlier by a large herd of horses. Though
the hoofprints were much trampled over, steaming piles of
dung told us unerringly what had passed before us.*

*Though I had not mentioned the need of steeds to the
Warlock, I felt that the movement of so large a number of
mounts must be in some way connected with our presence. I nodded again. The man was efficient, grant him
that. And he used his brain, which few monarchs ever
feel the necessity for doing.*

*The going was treacherous. Where it was not trodden, it
was deep and tiring. Where it was smoothed, it was icy
and slick. And, in less than an hour, we turned from the
roadway into the merest dimple in the drifts of snow.
Now it was a struggle, indeed, to make our way, but we
followed the young guide, and he never ceased the shrill
and tuneless whistling that had accompanied us all the
way.*

*We emerged into the relative snowlessness of a grove of
huge fir trees. Above, we could see that their thickly needled and massive branches held up a roof of snow, but the
needle-strewn soil underfoot held only occasional patches
of white. In the midst of the largest space was pitched a
tent of large dimensions.*

Our guide halted outside it and whistled once, very sharply. The tent-flap opened and a hand beckoned us in.

Now my companions had accompanied me many times upon such expeditions to contract our services. Never before had they been silent upon the road. Not once had I seen a look of unease on the face of Harl Indvor, yet now I saw a muted look of dread on all the faces about me. Still, we were here, and we must go forward.

Inside, the tent was lined with costly carpets. It was warmed by four braziers, set at the compass points, as nearly as I could reckon; appropriate, given the strange orientations of sorcerers. In the center of the carpeted floor stood a tripod holding a steam kettle that purred gently with its internal flame, filling the air with the fruity scent of wine. On a small table beside it were ten silver cups, each engraved with a different pattern.

We eased ourselves down, cross-legged, and waited for someone to appear. That happened soon enough, and in a way calculated to awe the ignorant. We managed to suppress our smiles as a curl of smoke coagulated beside the kettle, thickening into an opaque pillar. From the midst of this hokum stepped the tall shape of the Warlock.

We creaked to our feet again, as it is only meet to do when greeting a king. He smiled, a thin grimace, and motioned us down again, snapping his fingers for a servant.

There must have been another tent attached to the back of the one in which we sat, for a small, scared man trundled in and began pouring cups of steamy wine. The tallest he offered to his lord, and his hand trembled as it extended the cup. The next he gave to me, and I noted that its design held the face of a blindfolded goddess.

When all were served, the King lifted his cup, two-handed, and said, "Let us drink to the success of our mutual business. May you return home richer than you

came, and may I remain here more secure than I have
been from my enemies."

We drank, and the stuff was a bit too sweet and a bit too
hot. Suddenly, there in the closeness after the chill walk
in clean air, I felt myself becoming drowsy . . . almost
addled. But I fought my eyes open and steadied my wits
as best I could. I noticed that my fellows were blinking
and shaking their heads and shrugging deeply as if to
make themselves alert.

The Warlock read his agreement to us in a burring
voice that was drowsy as a bee in clover. Concentrate as I
would, the words blurred together into a comfortable
purr, and I found myself nodding agreement when the
King looked at me. At the last, after many grand words
about "ample remuneration" and "valuable services," I
heard one word that made my struggling spirit leap frantically for a foothold in reality.

". . . and sell them into slavery" . . . the voice
purred. But I could not hold onto the protest that rose in
me, and too soon I found myself signing the parchment,
along with the leaders of the men.

So it was that my mercenaries, fresh from the clean if
ambitious battles of the Krel, found themselves engaged
as slavers, to the bitter grief of all of us, saving only the
Rikkar, who thrive on such deviltry.

It was not death, after all. I came to myself, free of all
but the memory of pain (that, itself, leaves one sore and
weary). I was bundled in a rough blanket like that I had
bedded in during my years as a mercenary. A small fire
burned cautiously, fed just enough to keep it alight,
under a low embankment that curled slightly outward
directly above my head. Hunched over that tiny blaze was

Zorek, no longer armored but clad in leather and fur inner garments.

I stirred, and he turned and bent over me, his face still wary in the early morning light. "How is it that I live?" I asked him. "The Warlock meant my death—I could feel it in the thrust of his needle."

"There are more warlocks, and in more lands, than this," he replied. "In my work, we sometimes run afoul of such—or they are called in to counter us. A sorceress in Krel was my teacher in the damping of spells. She had come from a vast continent on the other side of the Blue Waters, where even Krel ships rarely venture, and she was a master of such lore. She cast spells of her own, too, of entirely another sort." He chuckled. "The waxen image is the commonest of instruments, used by even hedge-wizards. Countering the needle's thrust needs not even a real sorcerer, to my good fortune, as more than once I would have been sped by such means, myself."

I lay back, weary but no longer weak and sick. "Now, how did it come about that Zorek, the invader of my long-time principality, concerns himself with my welfare? You could have left me there to die without staining your sword with my blood."

"You made me think," he answered, shortly. "You asked why a ruler freely chosen would deliver his people over to enslavement. I was so busied with trying to wrest a fair wage from him for my men and for me that I did not consider the worth of his words, nor the logic of his reasons. After twenty years of shrewd bargaining with men of all stamps, I was befuddled by a petty Warlock sitting on a mountain! And not, I think, without the aid of some device."

"If you drank with him," I said, "there was good reason for your befuddlement. So did my father lose his kingdom, after drinking with the Warlock. He staked all on a single roll of the dice. And he lost. My father has a head that could match drink for drink with Cloud-Cap. No wine ever delivered by a vintner could sozzle him. So I knew that he had been . . . assisted into drunkenness. But I was young, impatient of the cares of learning to rule, wanting to marry a young woman considered unsuitable to be a future queen. I felt for my father, but I reveled in my own freedom. The Warlock could not conceive of anyone's giving up rule so lightly. He banned me and set a bounty on my head, then he sold my still-loyal people to you. They suffered and died because they hate the Warlock."

"I can see that it must be so," Zorek said. "I have only now had time to sit quietly and think through all that has been said and done since I had the misfortune to receive the Warlock's message. Would that I had never come into Lantirion."

"What do you intend to do, now that you have seen the truth?" I asked.

He carefully removed the fur cap that he had on his head, and for the first time I could see his face clearly. With a little cold breeze riffling his hair, he stood looking a bit upward, as if at the sky. His was a face that even the present winter had not robbed of its years of sunburn. Its scarrings wove white networks across his right cheek and his forehead. His blondish hair was cut across at the nape, and his startlingly pale brows crouched over ice-blue eyes that now looked down at me.

"I have never been squeamish about the tasks I undertook," he said. "If the pay was right, and my men agreed, we would accept almost anything that was offered in a fair bargain, fairly arrived at. But I have been lied to, not an unusual thing, but one I can ordinarily detect. I have been drugged into accepting a miserable bargain. I have gone against the will of most of my men, always excepting the Rikkar, who thrive on such doings as we have done. And I have lost my army as a result of the aforementioned lies.

"I have crossed blades with you, and you have only one equal, always barring myself. Harl was one who might have bested you. A warrior, so I surmise, who has suffered at the hands of this Warlock as you have, will have words to say to him. I do not know the way to his stronghold, for he met us secretly in Antri, but I am sure that you do know it. And I also have words to say to this Wizard who is so careful of his play that he must unbalance the dice in his favor. In more ways than one, I should think."

I grinned. Had he claimed a sudden affection for me, or had he suggested that he was of such nature that he could see no hurt man go unaided, I would have doubted him to my very bones. But he gave reasons that rang true, and I was nothing loath to have such a canny man and master warrior at my side. Courageous as my folk had proven themselves to be, I knew that they would be no match for the men and the methods that would face any who approached the Warlock's citadel.

CHAPTER 11

Mowen moved through the snow. It was deep . . . almost to her waist in places . . . but she never faltered in her steady progress. She had traveled from Antri northward in the shelter of the low-lying southern mountains, aided at every hut and farmstead by the generous folk who thickly populated the region. But when she came to the eastern skirt of the plains she looked out over an ocean of unbroken whiteness as pure as if no foot had ever been set there. A wind of biting iciness whipped down those long reaches, threatening to saw her ears from her skull, and she paused to prepare herself for the ordeal ahead.

She was clad in fur breeches and tunic, with fur-lined boots and a huge fur cloak that could double as a sleeping roll. Her hair was hidden under the woolen headdress that identified her order, and that, in turn, peeped from under a hood that could be let down to cover her face, leaving two slits for her to see through. Still, no furs ever grown by any beast could ward away from a lone traveler the vicious cold that the Warlock had laid like a scourge across the back of his lands.

So Mowen stood at the edge of the plains, a long arm of which cut her off from the eastern mountains that were her goal. Her training disciplines were unlike, perhaps, those of any religious order upon the globe of which Lantirion was one corner. She breathed deeply, flinging her cloak back to hang behind her, letting the hood drop also. With closed eyes, she stood in the stinging wind, letting the cold permeate her whole body, steal into the corners of her heart and mind.

"Cold, be my friend!" she chanted. "Be a part of me, my comfort and my shield. In the name of Him Who Calls Upon the Name, come into the house of my flesh and know it for your home, allowing it to move through your domain without hindrance. Move through me as I move through you, one and inseparable!"

She waited there, feeling herself move into the "other" state that she had practiced so often in the security of the Order. All sensation dulled away; there was neither warm nor cold, fear nor joy. She knew that she might walk for days, now, without hunger or weariness, though her body would demand a reckoning when she again allowed it to resume its normal condition.

Settling the cloak around herself again, she wriggled the heavy pack strapped to her back beneath the fur garment into a secure position. Then she set out across the untracked snow.

Halfway across that seemingly unbroken tract of whiteness, she came upon a broad, churned trail that told of men and horses passing that way since the last snowfall. The Guard, she well knew, lay in its winter quarters at Antri, quarreling and wenching and dicing away the untoward weather. This was the track, nevertheless, of an army. All the signs that she had learned to recognize in the unorthodox schooling of the Order were there to be read by the knowing.

"Nothing lies in the plains save the poor villages of the plainsfolk," she said aloud. "No army could find any enemy to attack there. Only the sheep in their hidden runs and the folk in their crude huts are to be found."

She gazed long at the wallowed trail, crossing her own as it moved out into the expanse of the open lands. Puzzled, she shook her head, feeling that she should follow, in order to find what the group looked for and who made up its numbers. But her orders had been specific.

"Mowen," the principal priestess had said, "He Who Calls Upon the Name has sent for me, this past morning, to attend Him at his house. There is work to be done, and only you have all the qualifications to do it. The priestess must be young and strong enough to travel through this unholy winter. This eliminates me and all the senior members of our Order.

"She must be versed in all the techniques and lore that we teach those who are to be our future directors and teachers. She must be of steadfast heart and sanguine nature, unshakable in her duty except by the hand of death itself. She must love Lantirion second only to the gods and to Him. You are the sole priestess in all the Order to have all the necessary qualifications.

"This is a task that may mean death . . . not only to you but to many in our nation. But it may well help to rid us of this mad Warlock who seeks to rule our folk with whips and hanging ropes."

When the Principal had fallen silent, Mowen had felt her face flush with excitement, and she had asked, "What must I do?"

"Go into the eastern mountains, even under the citadel of the Warlock himself. There you will find our old king, who is descending from his steep hiding place. His purposes were not revealed to me by Him, but the old man must be aided by one versed, as you are, in intricate and holy knowledge. You will come upon him above the forest line, which means that you must go up through the hills and make your way on the hem of the heights, keeping watch by dark and by day. When you find the king and his old huntsman, your way will become clear to you, moment by moment. Instructions now might cause you to lose the edge of inspiration that can come to a free mind. Follow your best instinct. Trust in the gods." The old priestess made the finger-circling motion of blessing, and kissed her forehead. And that had been the beginning.

Mowen shook her head and moved across the track, moving toward the forested hills that made a low, dark line across the horizon ahead of her. The mountains beyond them were lost in cloud that promised more snow to come, so she hurried, forcing her legs to terrible efforts. When night fell, the snow came, and she dug herself into a drift, leaving only a fist-sized hole to the outer air for ventilation.

She forced down a strip of dried meat, drank watered wine from her flask, though her stomach protested, subdued as it was by the force of her willing at the edge of the plain. Then she rolled herself into the cloak, pulling the hood down over her face. Inside that furry bundle, she was icy cold, but her flesh did not know it. Still, the protection of wraps kept her extremities from freezing into unusability, and so she had been taught to do. She wondered, drifting into a chill slumber, if it were a possibility that she might ever find some circumstance that had not been specifically dealt with in her long training. Then she slept.

When she woke, it was still snowing, so she settled back into her bolt hole, after surveying the outside world carefully. But nothing could be seen through the swirling blizzard, and she enclosed herself again and went into a light trance, waiting for the storm to abate.

As she hung in that suspended state, a face came before her inner eyes, and she gazed at it with interest. Red-gold hair looped about a pale, fine face with wickedly intelligent black eyes. A voice spoke to her mind, "You are Mowen, the priestess sent by Him Who Calls Upon the Name?"

"I am," she answered. "And you, if I miss not my guess, are Varil, the sorceress, beloved of Karas Lantir. I am about the business of the gods. What do you have to say to me?"

The glowing face laughed, a delightful chuckle that held neither awe nor dread. "You are arrogant, youngling, but that is all to the good, in the task you attempt. And do you think that the gods use only those from the Order in their works? How think you that He Who Calls Upon the Name knew that the old king had moved from his high place? I have kept my far gaze upon him, since he was sent forth from his own house. It was I who looked afar into the heart of Him and told Him how things stand."

Mowen, in her translated state, saw the words form in her mind, limned in gold like that of a good fire, and she also saw that they were true. "I am sorry," she said to Varil. "In the life I have lived, little of the actual outside world as it is at the moment comes to me. I see that I have misled myself in assessing you. What will you?"

"The track you crossed on the plain is that of slavers . . . yes, slavers, brought into Lantirion by the Warlock to punish the folk for their stubborn defense of the king and the prince. They are in the plains, even now, and tomorrow they will sweep away the villages within range. Then they will bring their captives back to the hills and camp there, waiting for those who have gone into the hills to bring in their own prisoners. Though you cannot, unaided, find your direction through the snowstorm, you must go up through Threll-mouth into the hills as soon as may be. I will guide you there, if you will follow my urgings." Varil sighed and waited for a reply, and the light on her skin flickered as if a fire burned high on a hearth before her.

"I will go," said Mowen. "Show me the way."

She burrowed out of her shelter and began plowing her way through the now higher drifts. Inside her head, Varil's voice came, now and again, saying, "Bear to the right more. You are tending to circle leftward." Or, "There is a deep drift ahead; go to your right fifteen paces, then turn back left, and you will miss it."

It was no easy—not even a possible—journey. Anyone, man or woman, untrained in the techniques Mowen used would have left a frozen corpse to stare away the winter until spring thawed the plains again to greenness. But her teaching had been thorough and painstaking, and her guide saw more than her own eyes would have been able to, even on a clear day. So when a second dawn broke through the eastern clouds, Mowen stood above the Threll and looked back along the way she had come.

"My trail may still be visible when the slavers come, if they move in this direction," she said silently to Varil, who had not left her during the whole journey. "The snow is becoming lighter."

"Go quickly, Mowen. There is shelter for you above the treeline, where you can relax your discipline, eat and drink and sleep without fear of cold or attack. But you must hurry!" Varil's command bore the weight of great urgency, and Mowen once again set her numbed limbs into motion, climbing through the deepening hills and the ever thicker forest.

She came out onto the northern instep of Cloud-Cap into darkness, but Varil's specific directions guided her to a hunter's hut just at the edge of the wood. There she found a goodly store of firewood, left there for such need as hers. Still using those inner-directed energies that she willed from herself, she built a fire, laying the logs so that the ends would fall into its center, keeping it alight past the normal life of a wood fire. She set an iron pot at its edge and filled it with snow and strips of dried meat and herbs from her pack, as well as some root vegetables left in the underground box in the corner of the hut.

Then she spread her cloak on the sheepskin before the fire and rolled herself into it. As she closed her eyes, she heard Varil say, "Fear nothing. We watch together, the gods and I, over your rest, for you must be strong and ready when you come to the side of the king. The seal of peace on your eyelids!"

Deep floods of sleep poured over her, and even that spark of self that had always kept watch for her seemed drowned in their dark waters. No dream troubled her, no apprehension of life or death.

She woke, many hours afterward, starved as a hunter boy, to find her fire died away to red coals, and her stew simmering in the pot over it. In comfort such as she had known little in her disciplined life, she sat before the blaze, dipping up the stew in her horn cup and drinking the broth, leaving the good meat to be picked out with her fingers. With a chunk of the hard bread from her pack, the food began the task of renewing her overstressed body. But she knew that she must rest for a day and another night before she could totally rely on her strength again.

CHAPTER 12

In the clear light of a new day, Mowen moved from her refuge onto the rock-strewn edge of the heights. Against the snow, even so small a thing as a dark bird could be clearly seen for great distances, and she was certain that she would not miss the old king and Grom, if ever they came into eyeshot. Varil had left her, her bright face shadowed by a fatigue so deep that she seemed sodden with it. But she had left behind one whom she could call friend as long as either of them lived.

Another day was spent in seeking, but that night Mowen could see a sharp point of red light against the breast of an adjoining eminence. She marked its direction well, laying a long staff toward it from the spot where she was camped, then she slept again, without unease.

Moving upward in the dawn, she could see, now and again, a small shape dark against the lightening sky, and by noon she could make out the forms of two men, both bundled to the ears in furs, both stooped with age or illness. When they saw her, they waved and hallooed, and she hastened to come up to them. And when she came to the spot where they waited, the King took her hands in his own, all bundled as both were in mittens, and kissed her cheek.

They sat on a wind-scoured boulder, there in the weak sun of a winter afternoon, and talked of their journeys and their purposes. Grom, wrinkled as a thorn root, sat glum and silent in disapproval of the entire proceeding, as his master looked out across the forested hills and over the plain and said, "We go to beard the Warlock in his den, daughter of holiness. We two are old and of no account. It ill becomes us to skulk in a hole in a mountain, however comfortably appointed, while one who has no right to it rules Lantirion. Our deaths will shake no stars from the firmament, nor will they overly distress us. Honor demands that I face that deceitful sorcerer and denounce him, man to man."

"You are in the right," answered Mowen. "But you have far more reason, now, than you did for such an action. The Warlock has banned your innocent son, placing a bounty on his head. He has sold your people to the Krel, through mercenaries acting as slavers. I have been sent by the gods, as well as by Him Who Calls Upon the Name, to stand beside you in your endeavor. More powerful interests than those of a king's honor waver in the balance of fate. I have been trained all my life to uphold the purposes of the gods."

The King shrank upon his stone, his mittened hands gripping his staff as if to squeeze it in two. "He has—sold my people?" he whispered, a quaver of anguish in his voice. "My folk are wearing the yoke of Krel, to be sold overwater like cattle? I shall shake the very mountain down upon that serpent!"

But Grom, so long silent, was now ready to speak. "You say truly?" he asked Mowen, looking closely into her dark eyes as if to wring the truth from them. "The folk of the hills and plains and of Antri are to be chattels? Then I am ready. We will go! Not until now have I seen a stone's worth of good in the prattle of honor, but this be another thing altogether. Up from the stone, Man King," he ordered his erstwhile ruler. "We go now!"

And the King rose . . . and stood straight as a young man, borne up by an anger as pure and hot as the boiling deeps of the mountain core that sent up hot springs and, sometimes, streams of molten rock from fissures in its side. He set off again, not downward now. He found paths that might have puzzled one of the native goats. He found hand and footholds that a gymnast would have distrusted. Faster than anyone would have dreamed, who had seen him before his meeting with Mowen, he led his unhesitating companions along the secret way that led to the Warlock's keep, shunning the guarded road that the Warlock had made upon the southern reach of his own mountain, Fire-Shouter.

Night fell before many hours passed, but in the short time they had traveled the three had drawn near to the very ridge that, when they reached its top, would allow them to overlook the Warlock's Citadel. They paused, then, and made a cold camp, chewing dried meat and sipping watered wine before sleeping. But all of them felt an unease, Mowen knew, for the old men groaned and gnashed their teeth as they slept, and she found it hard to close her eyes. She felt a searching mind casting back and forward across the jagged lands about them. The far-seeing power that Varil possessed in such wise clarity was also, in part, a talent of the Warlock, though his was far less acute, Varil had told her. Mowen sighed, then turned her mind to sleep.

But morning brought only an increased sense of being under surveillance to them all. Grom opened his eyes and said, "He looks for us, that old fox. He knows we hunt him, and he cannot find our spoor, as yet. Let him search! We will be upon him before he clears his eyes."

The old King smiled, a bit grimly, and said to Mowen, "This is a perilous venture, daughter. It is likely that none who walk with me into that lair of sorcery will ever walk out again. Heed my warning, and take thought for yourself."

But Mowen shook her head. "Whom the gods order into battle does not retreat at a word of danger. Still, that is not our immediate concern. Yonder searching wizard is plotting. I feel it. I sense it. I smell it. He has set some guard upon this whole mountain . . . a trap that is about to be sprung in hope of catching us unaware.

"So! I begin to see for what purpose I was sent to you. Quickly, slip farther into the cranny that sheltered us. Death rolls on the slopes!" And she hustled the two deep into the crack, setting her own back to the opening, as all now felt in the rock that held them the rumbling vibration they could not yet hear.

Ten long heartbeats passed, and the rumble became a growling roar that grew in volume until they crammed their fingers into their ears, feeling that their very brains would shatter in the terrible noise. The slit filled with dust, and pebbles and grits rained down on their heads, as they tried to make their flesh meld to the bone of the mountain.

For a long, long while, the mountain sloughed off its skin of rotted stone and loose scree. Breathing grew difficult, and Mowen could hear the old men coughing, even above the noise of her own. She grew afraid that the stresses of dust and noise and anger might be enough, of themselves, to snuff out those brittle lives. She prayed to the gods who held the weights of justice balanced in their chill hands that they might allow this small justice to be done, unimportant though it might seem in a universe that seemed to spawn chaos.

When, at last, the slide quieted, finding its angle of repose, the three were buried to the knees in small debris that had come to rest with them in their slot of rock. The slit that had given them access was gone, as was the ledge that had led to it. It seemed another mountain entirely that they stood upon, when they struggled painfully up the narrow cranny above them into the dust-dimmed light of day.

Below them lay a loosely sloping angle of rubble, still settling, here and there, in a puff of dust. Above them, much of the overhang of yesterday had been sheared away, and new chimneys scored the steep as with the claws of a hunting cat. But the way was passable. All of them knew it as they stood in the freshening air, and without words they began the climb to the roof of the ridge.

There were few encumbrances, now. Bedrolls had been left behind in the scramble for safety. Only their water jugs and food pouches were still strapped to their shoulders, as they remained at all times on the trail. The difficulty of the climb assured them that they were well rid of bulky items, for the old king made hard work of it, the starch of his anger a bit wilted by the ordeal of dust.

The rising sun was hidden behind a thin layer of cloud, and a cold wind whipped across their backs as they moved upward. Before night came, incredible as it might seem, they topped the ridge and made camp in the lee of it, sheltered from the wind. Hidden by the darkness, the Citadel of the Warlock lay on a level with them, across a cup-shaped valley, on the flank of the highest peak of Fire-Shouter.

No window opened outward from that fortress to let a chink of light escape. Light, like all else, was the Warlock's, locked tightly within his keep. Though they strained their eyes, none of the three invaders could find anything to mark its location, though they knew that it was there, a long day's journey away.

Sleep was a thing of brief necessity, done with as quickly as possible. First light saw them moving cautiously down the steep leading into the valley. Their watchword was wariness, remembering the slide of the day before, and Mowen found herself setting each hand and foot with quickened breath and rapid pulse, dreading to find herself slipping down the declivity in a tumble of rock.

Noon found them in the valley, picking their way down the narrow gullies that carried away the snow-melt in spring. The gullies were all but choked with snow, now, but they offered what cover there was to be had. Mowen did not relish the thought of traveling the breadth of that unmarked page of whiteness unsheltered from enemy eyes. Grom and the old King agreed, and they went far out of their way, keeping to meandering runs and washes. They were more comfortable when they came under the edge of the escarpment on which the Citadel was built. They felt that those who kept watch could see little, if they looked straight down, for all their furs were so caked with snow that they must be hard to see from any distance.

The old King, who had said nothing for so long that both his companions were beginning to feel concerned, now spoke. "There is a cavern, here someplace. I roamed these mountains as a boy, before ever the Warlock was conceived or his keep built. Unless the quakings and rumblings of these old heights have closed it up, it leads back into the face, then upward by way of holes like to chimneys. Many a wild goat I have felled on yon height, watching across the valley with its strange eyes for any enemy, when one had risen secretly from the very ground behind it. If the ways I remember still lead upward, we can go up into the Citadel itself, provided they have not sealed over the hidden outlet with some cornerstone or block."

He moved along the snow-covered foot of the cliff, peering closely at every hole and cranny. It grew dark, but the snowlight made a bit of light to fumble their way by. And they found the cave, a slight-seeming depression, to begin with, that widened into a low tunnel, that, in turn, opened out into a chamber large enough for a Great Hall. Against one wall they camped and built a fire using the fragments of wood left, all those years before, by the King on his rambles and hunts about the heights.

Mowen lay back against a rock and gazed into the fire. For the first time since leaving the hunter's hut, she was warm and fed, though scantily. Her eyes felt heavy, and she was on the point of drifting into sleep when the face of Varil looked out at her from the coals.

"Well done!" said that bright image. "You are coming, all three, to the very edge of your great endeavor. And help will be with you, when need arises. Go confidently. I cannot hold long, for you are under the mountain, though not too far, else I could not reach you at all. Hold fast, keep courage, and trust in the gods!" And her face winked out with the last of the embers.

"Did you see?" whispered Mowen, and the King answered, "Yes, daughter. She who was denied her place by those who now court favor with my enemy has watched over me, I have known. Now she moves along her own strange road in our aid. I have much—much to regret."

They slept for a time, but there being no chance of a dawn, they rose before long and fashioned torches from the tinder-dry stuff the young King had used in his wanderings. A spark from the striker that Grom kept always with him kindled one to light, and they moved down the tunnel, keeping the faint, fresh breeze in their faces. It seemed that they walked for hours, kindling a fresh torch from a spent one, winding and climbing and scrambling along the gut of the mountain.

When the last torch flickered and died, Mowen felt an instant of panic, the weight of the whole planet seeming to fall upon her with the blackness. As she struggled to regain her control, the voice of the old King sounded through the darkness, "Fear not. Seldom, when I was young, did I trouble myself to make a light. I knew the ways so well that I did not often trouble myself with torches or a lightglass."

Mowen felt her hand taken, and she reached back and felt for Grom, who caught her mittened hand in his wiry grip. Carefully, feeling for secure footholds, they climbed a mound of rubble, then went down its other side. There, the floor was smoother, and walking was less chancy, with only a shruff of dust sounding beneath their heels.

"It has changed," mused the King, "but not so much— no, not so much as I. A few daggers of rock have fallen from the roof, and a few boulders lie on the floor that were not here before, but the shifting of the world in its long sleep accounts for that. No foot has been put here, I know, since I last was here. There is no smell of mankind left in these deep ways." His voice died away, to be followed into silence by strange, muttering echoes.

Then he halted, and all felt the chill freshness of air gushing down onto the tops of their heads. They looked up, but no glimmer of light was to be seen. Still the King loosed his hand from Mowen's, and she could hear him feeling about in the darkness. After a time, he called softly, "Ah!" There was a grating sound, a slithering, and he spoke again, near to hand.

"My friends, I have found my old road. It is a difficult one, but you both are strong and determined. First we must climb this ledge before us." And he guided Mowen to the place and she groped about, feeling for a way to climb it. As she went up the sharp slant, she heard the others coming behind her.

Atop the pile, the draft of air was strong, sucked swiftly away to flow out the long way they had come. Mowen reached above her head and felt blindly for the opening into the chimney. It was there, and she moved higher, set her elbows into a groove, and began edging her way up, using knees and back to hunch her way upward. The sounds below told her that her companions were painfully following her example, and she knew that their aching bones and stiffened muscles must be an agony to them.

The breeze became almost a gale, and she wondered why it flowed so, downward into the deeps. But when she emerged from the stringent slit at the top of her climb, she knew. The winds that blew steadily from the west, across the valley, funneled here into a sort of bay in the rock of the mountainside. The slit was at the throat of that funnel, carrying the strong wind down. And the door of the Warlock's stable faced her, as she stood staring about her.

She drew back into the bay, behind one of the curling lips that all but hid it from the stableyard below. She felt certain that the old King knew much more about the arrangements of the Warlock's keep than did she, and she set herself to wait for the two who came behind.

With much harsh breathing and moans of effort, the King came into view, rising from the hidden crack as if by magic. He was closely followed by Grom, and when they stood together in the concealment of the bay, he looked well pleased.

"They dug away much of the debris that lay in a long slope downward from this place," he said, "leaving my secret doorway not only unblocked but actually invisible from ground level. You can see that they used the gravels from the pile to surface the stableyard and the paths. And look away yonder around the edge of the Citadel . . . there goes the road he built to Antri, along the eastern reaches of these mountains. They say he used sorcery to move the soil and stone of the roadway into place, for none of our folk would labor for him. I think that he probably hired the Krel to work it for him with their slaves. His sorcery is not so strong a thing as he would have us believe."

Mowen gazed across the grounds of the Citadel, then she turned and said, "Well, King, we are here. What now?"

He chuckled, a dry sound like stubble rustling in the wind. "Now we walk where we cannot be and say what no man dares to say to a wizard. Come, my friends, let us use the kitchen door, as it is so convenient to our needs. An ex-King need not stand on his dignity, I think." And he laughed aloud, but quietly, and led the way down the short drop to the stableyard.

They alighted in a squabble of geese and a flap of hens, but no one came to investigate the babble. Only a black charger thrust his head from his loose box to whinny at them. Answering whinnies from down the row of stalls told them that many fine animals were stabled there.

"He has called in his sycophants," the king whispered. "All those who thought to prosper by our downfall came scraping and purring about him, when I left the throne to him. Now I'll wager they are all here, called in for some scheme of his. His personal household numbers few who can call themselves noble in any way, and most of those are of such inferior houses that pure-blooded horses are outside their interests or experience."

Grom grunted, scraping poultry dung from his hide boot as he prepared to climb the curving stone steps to the entryway. "Say it plain," he advised. "Cackle pates fit to make those in the yard look wise as seers. Coattail clingers, every one, falling over themselves to please their mighty Warlock, but fearful as sneak thieves to walk out in Lantirion for the *real* folk to spit at."

Now they stood at the back entrance of the Warlock's castle. A straight hall let a generous draft of icy air sweep through the rear offices of the building, for the heavy wooden door stood open, propped with a stone. Damp patches were rapidly drying on the stone flags, and a woman so old her wrinkles were being erased by the shrinkage of her flesh to the skull beneath crouched over a bucket of filthy water, nursing her knotted hands in her apron and moaning softly.

Mowen felt anger surge hotly through her, and she stepped softly to the woman's side and said, "Old Mother, go to the kitchens and warm yourself. No more will you scrub cold flags in dire weather. Wrap yourself in your shawl and sit by the fire until I come again to speak to you."

Dim eyes looked up at her fearfully. "Who'm be ye?" she quavered. "M'm got te finish the hall, else they'm beat me!"

"Go to the kitchens," said Mowen, her eyes flashing and authority in her voice. "No one will beat you, I promise."

As the woman shuffled off down the hall and into an

arched doorway on the right, Grom cursed savagely. "Ahoris's mother, that 'un! Good old besom, she always was, to any as came. And her son a loafing, lackadaisical do-nothing. Likely he sits turning a spit, here, stealing snippets of meat, never thinking of what he's brought his old 'un to!"

But the King didn't wait to listen. His head was up, his chin set, and years seemed to have fallen from him, as he started decisively up the steps that led from the cross-hall into a short corridor that ended in a door banded in iron.

"Good spies earn their pay," he mused, as he fumbled in his pouch. "Those that live, that is. I lost three before one was able to bring me this." And he drew forth an intricately fretted key that slid silently into the big keyhole that centered a brass embellishment. It turned, and they found themselves in a wide hall, richly hung with paintings and tapestries, that curved gently out of sight both right and left.

"We go thus," he whispered. "I know this keep as though I had drawn its plans and walked every day with its builders. I have sat long on the hills, but I have not been idle. I memorized all I could find, recalled things I had forgotten, and now I know the way."

He turned to the right, and Mowen moved at his heels, feeling Grom's presence behind her, though his hunter's feet made no sound at all. A few paces down the corridor, just around that gentle bend, was an ornate door that had been set waist-high from the level of the floor. To it led circular steps that shone with a deep red light as if they were cut from jewel stone. The door echoed the red, its panels being inset with thin slices of the same stone, through which the light on the other side shone with a somewhat sinister effulgence.

The King set his hand to the panel, and it opened before him as if it had awaited his touch. "I give you blessing, stone of the far hills," he said, making the looped circle of Riha, goddess of honest steadfastness, upon it with his finger. The door groaned and fell into dust, leaving the panels of red stone lying, broken free, on the floor.

He walked in as a king should, quietly and with total assurance. His companions did no less, and the wizard looked up from his concentration on a sphere of clear crystal to find himself being studied, in turn, by three sets of eyes whose clarity and lack of fear struck him cold to his hidden heart.

Through the seeing senses of Varil
The Citadel lay silent about the Warlock's study. Those who dwelled there by his favor had scurried to their rooms, stung by his rage into the panicked flight of children. Now he stood again beside the great window. This time the valley was filled with the dismal light of snow clouds, for they loomed over the line of peaks to the west. If he had possessed the power, he would have filled the skies with whirlwinds, for he had looked afar, deep into the hills, and while the villages lay empty, he had seen the forces of the mercenaries returning empty-handed to their leader.

Some force walked there, thwarting his will. Even now, he mulled bitterly over the terrible battle that he had seen upon the knees of Cloud-Cap. Little did he care for the guttered blood of the men who fell beneath the merciless stones. The fate of those he used was nothing to his chill heart. But citizens of Lantirion stood free upon the heights, unenslaved and unslain. Those whose captivity in the plains he had watched and gloated over were now freed of the snare he had set for them.

He was filled with gall as he moved to his cabinet and

took out a vial of red powder, a dish made of horn, and a crystal that had been shaped into a sphere. Shaking a little powder into the dish, he touched it into flame, and thick reddish smoke curled upward, filling the room with a lung-thickening stench.

Bent over the dish, he breathed deeply, until his thin frame was wracked with coughing. Then he set a lid over the dish and drew the crystal forward. He gazed deeply into it, straining his will to see.

A shape moved in the distances. It had stood on the height with those who rolled the stones. It now moved across the forest with a spark that could only be Zorek. Yet the shape was none of the mercenary's own. It was maddeningly indistinct, as if a veil were drawn between his inner seeing and the reality who inhabited that form. The aura it sent afar was none that he had ever encountered. Yet he knew it. He knew it.

The day wore toward noon, and he still gazed into the sphere. No comfort was to be found there. Indeed, the entirety of his stolen kingdom seemed to be filled with threat. Since he had thrust to kill Lantir, though he had sensed no stirring of the son of the King in weeks, he had been filled with dread. For something had thrust backward along the line of will. His needle had broken in his hand. The image had crumbled quietly into granules of wax.

Concentrated on the distant peak where the freed plainsmen were, he had neither time nor energy left with which to look nearer to home. So it was that he looked up from his work into the eyes of the King, of Grom, and of Mowen, as they quietly entered his strongest and safest sanctuary.

He seemed frozen for a moment, his back bent, his

chin lifted. Then he stood erect, his hands at his sides, his eyes glittering with reddish fires.

"You think to face me down, here in my own place, surrounded by the instruments of my power?" he asked, his voice incredulous. "Fools! You will learn, now, of the thing you attempted!"

His hand arced up, then down, and a shattering bolt of energy spurted toward the old King.

Mowen moved her hand in a pattern as intricate and inevitable as the precession of the equinoxes. The bolt was halted as if by a wall, the crash of its impact shaking the Citadel to its foundations. There was an instant of utter stillness, as the Warlock gazed at the girl with astonishment.

Into that quiet came the sound of distant shouts and screamings. Mowen gazed serenely back into the eyes of the sorcerer, her hand at the ready against any motion on his part. Though his own hands made no motion, the next bolt found her ready, weaving her protective pattern almost before it was aloft.

Time slowed to a crawl. Like some weird duel of sword against shield, the battle went on, bolt against pattern, crash after crash after crash shaking loose the mortar from the stones about them. None there knew when the sun went down behind the western heights, for they were locked will to will, eyes to eyes, hand to hand, in battle more dire than any that might be waged with mere blades.

Mowen stood straight and calm, deflecting danger from the King with an unwavering hand. Yet as the second day faded into dusk she grew weary. Her hand moved more slowly, and her back lost the slightest fraction of its straightness. Then Grom moved up behind her and placed his gnarled hand on her shoulder.

"Take from me, Daughter," came his gruff voice in her ear. "I've no skill in such warfare, but strength I've got, if I be ever so old. Draw upon it."

Then she straightened, and a tinge of color came into her pale cheeks. Her hand moved freely again, and the bolts quivered across the pattern, leaving faint tracings of color and form across the empty air.

About them, the walls began to show the faintest of cracks, and a little rain of dust began to trickle from the domed roof high above. The sounds of hurrying steps came and went down the hallways, as those who dwelled there fled to safety.

Once, indeed, there came the tramp of armored men along the corridor at their backs, and a dozen men moved to mount the steps to the doorway. The old King, however, drew out his blade, bright and thin with a generation of honing, and stood across the door.

"You may not enter here," he said, and those who stood below looked into his face. They knew him, every one, for their rightful ruler. They knew their sorcerous master for what he was, a source of unjust loot and ill-got wealth. They remembered Eliar, who had not come back again from his errand into the snow. So they bent their heads and turned on their heels and clanked away into the darkness of the hallway.

They stood, those three, amid a hailstorm of force. They endured, as night followed day and another dawn pursued it across the sky. And it seemed as though there would be no end to the Sorcerer's murderous bolts, no end to Mowen's marvelous patterning.

CHAPTER 13

The morning brought me to full vigor, after the stresses of battle with both Zorek and the Warlock's needle. Zorek's niggardly fire warmed us a stingy broth, flavored with fir tips, and we set about readying ourselves to make our way back to the foot of Cloud-Cap.

"Will those of your people who are left seek to stay or to stop your going with me?" I asked Zorek, and he laughed deep and long.

"Not those!" he chuckled. "They are the ragtag and bobtails of an army. Not a warrior or even a would-be warrior among them. They run errands, catch horses, boil mutton, tumble in the blankets with the first and last comers, according to their aptitudes and sex. I told them to set their faces to northward for Krel, else your sheepherders would stone them to rags. They took me at my word and are gone, every slacker and slattern of them. Loyalty, even among those who fight, is not so common among mercenaries as among settled folk. Nonexistent might fairly term it."

"Then let us move," I said, settling my small pack and moving my sword-sling convenient to my hand. "Before the day wanes, I would like to be on the slopes, for it comes to me that I am needed, up there where the Warlock dwells among the clouds in majesty. With you and Shal and Grem and Harl" . . . he started at that name, and I grinned at him. "Aye, Harl came to me, after we fought one another to the arms of exhaustion, even as did you and I. He hated slaving with every fiber of his northern flesh, and he was on his way, when we met. I seem to have a strange facility for turning enemies into allies. My luck, be warned, is either demonic or a gift of the gods."

"Better demons than warlocks," he grunted, swinging his pack to his shoulder and striding out of the sheltered spot to which he had brought me.

The sky seemed, for once, to have exhausted its immediate supply of snow, for the sky was a thin blue, in spots, though streaked with cloud and still carrying that cutting wind that dipped across the backs of the hills and made the bones ache. This made dawdling an unattractive thing, though, and we made fine time, moving up through the timbered hills toward Cloud-Cap. And, as I had hoped, we reached the steep slopes by nightfall. I knew that a few hours of the next morning would see us at the gory battleground.

It was, actually, almost midmorning when we came out into that still blood-splashed spot. The snow had been trampled into nothingness by the many comings and goings of our own folk and by Zorek's army, so there was no softening of the terrible reality of the death that had pounded men to mush. I laid my hand on Zorek's arm, but he shook my hand away and stood for a moment, staring blindly at the rust-stained rock of the cliff.

"They were good men—good fighters," he said at last. And that was their only epitaph, though I had many thoughts about the strangeness of fate that had led them to die here, uselessly, in pursuit of goals that most of them hated and despised. But I said nothing, just hallooed the weird wail that was the signal agreed upon.

When the answering wail came from above, I began

climbing, and Zorek came with me, almost alongside but a few arm's lengths away. We didn't speak, even when one or the other of us slipped and all but fell. The bond between us was such a hair-balanced amalgam of anger and respect and mutual need that both of us, I think, feared to set it swinging. But by the time we reached the ledge we had worked off the worst of our unease.

Harl was waiting for me, and great was his surprise when he hauled up his old commander as his first catch. But he said nothing as he locked his huge hand about my wrist and swung me up beside him on the ledge.

I looked about with amazement. "You have worked like heroes," I said. "You have left neither dead nor wounded below, and I can see that all our own dead are back in their place. Never have people achieved so much, I think, after being so sorely tried." And truly, the neat cairns that covered our own were again in place, as though their tenants had never made one last attack upon their enemies.

"We took Zorek's dead," and he nodded briefly toward my companion, "and laid them in a crevasse that cuts about the foot of the mountain, just around to the south. We covered them over with stones, that they might lie easy. Shal knew of the place—he is a mine of useful things, that one—and led us to it. As for the rest, you may thank Renath. She has chivied us all to great efforts. And now she has chivied them all toward food and rest, leaving me to chill my weary bones here, waiting for you."

I nodded gravely, though I knew quite well that neither blade nor threat would have moved him from that spot until I returned. The big northerner had, quite simply, found in me one whom he could trust and follow, without fear of betrayal. Some inner sense that few men come to know had waked in both of us, telling us that we were fate-bonded, more than kin. I clapped him on the shoulder and said, "Well, now you can go take your rest, Harl, and Renath cannot say you nay."

The climb was not so difficult, now that we had reached the crannied face, and I went up in good time, hearing all the while the sounds of two climbing beside me. We were greeted at the top by Shal and Grem and the indomitable Renath, who seemed to feel a proprietary concern for Harl that made me chuckle inwardly. They had us washed and freshly clothed (those practical folk, used to living on the edges of existence, had no qualms about taking from the dead what they no longer needed), fed full and sitting at ease before a roaring fire almost as quickly as I can set my quill to tell it.

We talked long into the night, even weary as we were, with folk sleeping the sleep of exhaustion all about us. Only one fire could be maintained, so long and difficult was the climb for a wood-laden person, and all slept rolled in whatever they could find in the one chamber where the nip of winter's teeth could not penetrate.

"The field packs of the army," said Renath, with an apologetic glance at Zorek, "were of great help to us. They were full of blankets and dried fruits and meats. And the cooks, when they ran away, left stews boiling over their cook fires. What the stones did not overturn, we salvaged, and you had some for your supper. Suitably seasoned by *real* cooks."

"And excellent fare it was, particularly to men as hungry as we. But now we must make plans for tomorrow, for there is much to be done, both on the mountain top and in the hills below," I answered, turning to Shal. But Zorek held up his hand, and I waited on his words.

"Before you begin wondering why your enemy sits among your councils, let me make my position plain to you. I was ensorcelled by yonder Warlock, else I would never have made the bargain I did. I do not claim that I would never have gone slaving. Given enough profit and the agreement of my men, I might have done it without thought or conscience. But I had no agreement from those of my men who were not Rikkar (I hope all of those lie dead), and I had no profit fit to take the name.

"Dull-witted from his deceits, I did as the wizard ordered me to do, forcing my unwilling companions to live with the result of my ill trading. They were on the point of rebellion, I think, when your force came down on us beside the stream. Now I am awake again, to my full wit and wrath. I will have words with yonder sorcerer if I must go alone, wandering the mountains until I find him. But Karas Lantir faced me in combat and showed himself my equal—and more. He showed himself a man and a noble, courageous and courteous alike. And I have joined myself with him, for now, so that we may both have our vengeance.

"If the day comes when our interests diverge, I will warn him—and you—in good time. Until then, I make bond to be a true comrade."

They glanced across our half-circle, Shal and Grem and Harl and Renath, exchanging unspoken comments. The past few days had welded us all into such closeness as is seldom come upon, even within family bonds, and we knew, most of the time, what the others thought, simply by the set of a jaw or the twitch of a shoulder. Now they agreed, without words, and Harl turned to me.

"I have known Zorek for six years, Karas Lantir. I have never known him to lie. I trust him . . . until he says to trust him no more." The big man held out his hand, and Zorek reached to grip it in the complex double-wrist clasp of the mercenary.

In turn, each of the others took his hand, and so the

pact was sealed with him who had been our enemy and enslaver against him who was, in very truth, the enemy of all of us.

"Now we must lay plans quickly, for we must all sleep," I said. "Renath, I leave to you the care of the folk here. When it seems that all are able to move, go down into the hills and seek out enough villages for all until all are able to return to their homes. Then send out criers. Have them say, 'Karas Lantir says to Adalla, come out of hiding. Bring with you all who are in secret places, for the enemy is no more among us.' And send them out every day until those who hide begin to come in. They will know how to reach those that the criers cannot."

She nodded, her weathered face warm in the firelight, and said, "I will care for all your folk, Karas Lantir, until they reassemble and can care for themselves." In the shadows, her hand crept toward Harl on the bench on which they sat, and I saw his big paw cover it.

"Shal, you and Grem and Harl, I will need with me, for we go to attack the Warlock himself. An army could not come upon him secretly, for armies need provender and time for rest and all those luxuries that we who are hardened to the hill life do not. We can go swiftly up the mountains, over the ridges, onto the shoulders of Fire-Shouter himself. And I surmise that the snows are not so deep upon the Warlock's own doorstep as upon the lands of those who oppose him. If that is so, we can walk into his door in three days' time."

They grunted assent, and Zorek nodded. "A quick, secret blow, struck by chosen men. That is the way I have won many a victory that otherwise might well have been a defeat. I am with you."

When all were rolled in their blankets before the banked fire, I sat awhile, gazing into the few winking coals. And again Varil took form before me, her red-gold hair warming the space about her more than any blaze ever could.

"Karas, my love, you have done well. Never would any have believed that our simple folk of Lantirion could destroy an army with stones! Those who whine about the heels of the Warlock would shiver to learn that you have made a friend of this enemy. But there is much to do, and quickly. See!" And into my mind she poured a sequence of visions, of the priestess Mowen moving through the snows, her finding my father and Grom, and their journey to the Citadel. The last vision seemed to freeze in time, leaving the three of them standing in the doorway, staring at the hunched figure over the crystal sphere. A feeling of terrible tensions that built to some weird explosion of forces left my hair crawling on my neck.

"Some of this that you witness has already taken place. This is, in part, a vision of things that will happen to them in the days just ahead. Even now, they are on their way. You must come to the keep within a day after they confront the Warlock, or none of them may survive the encounter. Though he is not so wonderful as a wizard, he is both shrewd and well-attended, little though it may seem so in the ease of your father's approach to him. And that way of approach is now open to you. Take heed!"

She winked out between breath and breath, and I sighed and lay back, feeling as if I and all my people were pawns on some tremendous game-board on the knees of the gods. Surely, we must hurry! And I dropped off to sleep and dreamed of a terrible journey.

CHAPTER 14

The journey was fully as terrible as the one I dreamed. Though it snowed no more, a wind that cut through fur and leather and skin to the bone beneath blew steadily over the heights. We were all skilled at moving over snow, and we had been provided by the canny Harl with frames of bent saplings, lashed together with strips of leather, that fitted to our feet and strapped onto them, allowed us to move over the surface rather than sink into the drifts.

"In my own land," he said, "drifts grow so deep that none might walk abroad in winter, to hunt or to trade, without using such. The need for going higher in the snows made me think that they might be good to have."

Of course, they were a nuisance in climbing, making it necessary to carry one more thing strapped to our already burdened backs, but they sped us up and down the rolling ridges with unheard-of rapidity. They made such a difference, indeed, that we came out into the other end of that valley into which the cavern-passage opened on the mark of noon of the second day from our setting out.

I could see the toothed ridge over which my father must have led his companions—the gods grant that it was not too long ago. I could see clearly the ragged verge of the cliff to which we must find our way. With only a short halt for a bit of food and a sip of watered wine, we donned our strange footgear and moved down the slopes with the peculiar gait that the frames demanded, if one were to keep both feet moving in the same direction. Well before night we came up against the cliff and began our search for the unobtrusive mouth of that cavern into which my father had gone.

I recognized it at once, when I came at last to the proper spot. I called softly, my voice echoing dimly in that cupped place, and soon my four companions joined me. Inside, we found the remains of the wood that my boy-father (how strange that seemed!) had brought there so very long ago. Though we were supplied with light-glasses foraged from the packs of Zorek's men, we also made torches, not relishing the thought of trying to find our way in the dark (by the sole light of my little sun), as my father had done. We had not his thorough knowledge of the underground ways.

Our trek was little different from that of those who had gone before us. We saw their dropped torch-stubs, and the sight cheered us, for we knew that, for good or ill, this evil game in which we were all caught up was drawing to an end. As we moved upward through the chimney, I found myself grinning, not with joy but with a sort of desperate anger at the fate that set two aged men and a young woman face to face with that devious villain, while I come tardily behind them.

When I emerged from the hidden slit at the top, I moved warily to the lip of the bay and looked down. Peaceful the stableyard may have been when Mowen first saw it, but it was no longer. It was a moil of half-dressed house guards, half-armored horsemen struggling to saddle their mounts, yelling servants—and hangers-on of the Warlock's court. The latter were quite obviously trying their best to find a way to leave the Citadel with as much speed as possible.

Motioning my companions to stay out of sight, as they

joined me, I listened past the cackle below. Then I noticed that my hair was trying, despite my helm, to stand erect on my head. The little hairs on my arms and legs were prickling upward. Strange tensions surrounded me, and from some place not too far away I heard terrific crackles followed by shattering noises, one after the other at intervals of a few breaths.

I guessed that even now the Warlock was engaged in battle with my father and Grom and Mowen. It ill-befitted his son to skulk in a hole in a hill while he did it. So I stepped into full view and looked down on the rabble below.

"Get you gone!" I shouted. "Karas Lantir has come to reclaim his own. Any who remain here will be like to die here!"

A surprising number did not even look up to verify my statement. They tore away, afoot or ahorse, down the road, which I saw was only lightly dusted with snow. But some twenty, mounted and in full armor, stood their ground, and I leaped down, sword drawn and dagger ready, to disrupt them before they could organize some defense.

I heard the light thuds as my companions landed behind me, and we advanced upon the Guard (I now saw that they wore the serpent-shield that was the Warlock's insignia). It was chancy work, for a mounted man has weight and reach far in excess of that of a foot soldier. And the sounds that came from the Citadel were reaching shattering volume. So I chose, then and there, to throw away my old reluctance to use strange abilities instead of good steel. Calling to the others to run for the kitchen door, I reached back onto the cliffside and hefted a pair of good-sized boulders.

My practice in the caverns, weeks and weeks ago, had

been a good thing. Now I could set those weights in motion, aim them just as I wanted them, and then leave just a portion of my mind to see them through their task, while the rest of me attended to other things.

The eyes of all the mounted men were on us five. None looked upward until the first boulder struck the right arm of the crescent into which they had drawn, smashing three men with their mounts. Then the rest looked up—to see another, even larger rock sailing down the sky at them. They scattered, but it was too late. Six more were struck, more or less heavily, while the rest set out to catch up with those who had fled earlier.

All five of us were safely within the kitchen entry, at work on the heavy door (it was now closed and barred from within) by the time the second rock stopped rolling. Inside, I could hear a muted babble of voices, and I guessed that the servants were there, perhaps with a footman or two who might be armed. And I refused to waste time on anything so irrelevant as a door. I aimed the force of my will at that heavy and iron-studded leaf and fought to tear it outward.

It refused to move at all. It felt, to that strange sense of mine, as if it were engulfed in a sticky morass, sucked into place and immovable. I guessed that the Warlock had enspelled it, and I turned to find a quicker point of entry.

We went to the outward curve of the belly of the keep. Only a narrow way lay between the wall and the outward battlements that had been needlessly thrown up to guard against an impassable drop to the valley far below. The keep wall was unbroken, seemingly, and the outer wall was too far away to allow a leap to the roof from its top.

While I pondered, Zorek called, "A window! Come!" and I hurried after him, Shal, Harl, and Grem close at my heels.

High in that curving wall was one slit window. From our angle, we could not see if it was barred, but I assumed that it was.

"Stand behind me," I told my companions. "I will remove any grillwork that may be there." And once again I pulled against a resisting barrier . . . but this time it moved, grated against my pull, moved again, and fell with a clatter to the graveled path before us. An ornate grating, seemingly for decoration, but a strong one nonetheless.

"How will we climb?" asked Shal, measuring the distance with his eyes.

"We will not," I answered, leaning against the stone and breathing deeply, renewing my energies. "I will lift you four up, one by one. You must stand, two of you, just inside, so that when I appear you may catch me and pull me in. I will be unable to see when I reach your level."

Without waiting for a reply, I hoisted Grem with my nonphysical strength and set him upon that almost-invisible ledge. As the sun sank, I lifted each by turn and they clambered into the chamber that lay beyond the slit. Then I looked at the ground between my feet and pushed it away from me, slowly at first, then with more confidence as I felt my feet leave the surface and saw the pebbles grow smaller. I rose up that wall like a shadow, and Harl reached out his long arm and hauled me into the embrasure, when I reached that level.

We stood in a chamber that would have been quite dark, but for the red shaft of sunlight that peered from under the western edge of the mat of cloud that covered the sky, straight through the slit window. It was a record room of sorts; its walls were lined with scroll-laden shelving, and its limited floor space crowded with one large table that was covered with maps and charts and finely lettered parchments. There was a half-open door in the

wall opposite the window, and through it came the spit-
tings and cracklings and boomings of that terrible uproar
that had not ceased since we first heard it from the bay in
the mountainside.

Harl and Zorek slipped to either side of the casement,
Shal and Grem took up positions to either side and
behind me, and I pushed the door outward, slowly and
with caution. I need not have troubled myself. The uproar beyond covered any sound we might make, bar
rolling a boulder into the chamber. And the Warlock was
too intent upon the sorceries he was making to heed even
that.

It was a fantastic picture that met our eyes. The huge,
round room, vaulted to a great height and finished in
black and gold hangings, was shot through with lightnings. Before the door in the farther wall stood my father,
looking as he used to look when I was a boy and he a man
in his prime. Grom stood sturdily beside him, grasping his
stick in one gnarled hand and looking both bored and
amused, as was his wont in times of crisis.

In front of them stood a slight figure, even bundled as
it was in furs. Mowen's face was white, almost, as the
snow in the valley, and she seemed ready to drop with fatigue, but her hand moved steadily, inscribing a pattern of
loops and lines upon the air in front of her. That pattern
seemed to form a strange shimmer, like glass, in the air between the three and the Warlock, and against it rained
bolts of weird energy that hissed and cracked and boomed
upon it. But none of that deadly rain went through to
touch any who stood behind the protection.

The Warlock's back was toward us as he hunched over a
long table. Between his arm and his side, I could see a
shimmer of crystal, and it seemed that the lightning was
issuing forth from that. As we sidled along the wall, his

profile came into view, intent and concentrated upon the bright sphere that twinkled and shot forth bolts between his braced hands.

Even then, he did not see us. All his strength, every cell of his flesh and all his energy seemed directed through that sphere into the attack he was waging on the shield that protected the three by the door. I think that he would not have known that we were there had we walked up behind him and tapped his shoulder, so engrossed was he in his battle.

But Mowen was drained. I could see it in the effort it required for her to lift her weary hand and move it in the recurrent pattern. Her face had gone away to whiteness, leaving only two dark wells of eyes that shone steadfast, while her flesh drooped beneath them.

"We must hurry to them," said Zorek, at my side. "She is too weary to hold the spell."

With one accord, the five of us broke across the chamber, ducking stray bolts and sparks as we ran. When we reached the shield, we split into two parties and went around either side, coming behind it with the three already there. And as if our strength were added to her own, Mowen straightened her bowing shoulders and lifted her chin. Her hand moved freely, and the pattern shimmered a glazed wall before us, roofing away the rain of deadliness. Zorek stepped up beside her and echoed her motions.

She faltered for one heartbeat, with sheer astonishment, then she took up the pattern again, and his fingers faithfully copied hers until the motion was perfectly matched. Then he touched two fingers of his left hand to her wrist and pressed it three times. She looked up at him with wonder and gratitude and let her hand drop. The shield did not falter, though Mowen fell in a small heap at Grom's feet.

I lifted her and Grom spoke. "I will set her behind me, Princeling. She has been a rock and a shelter to us old 'uns. The Wizard would have blasted us from the ways of the world with one burst of yon lightning, had she not been with us to ward it off. For a night and a day—aye and part of the day before that—she has stood there battling yon Warlock. If old bones have any good left in un, I'll see mine serve her so long as they will move to my will."

I passed her light form back to him and turned to see how Zorek fared. He stood there, his face set in a strange smile, weaving the signs into the air with the confidence of one long used to such things. That shield was strong and enduring, I could see at a glance.

Then I checked behind us, for I like to know who can come at my back. Where tall doors had stood was a drift of dust and two long red stones. I peered through the gap down the corridor, but no one was in sight. A chuckle at my elbow turned me about, and I found myself facing my father.

"None will attack from the rear, my son," he said. "One or two came around the corridor far enough to see the lightning and to hear the thunder, and that small taste of the activities here sent them scuttling without further investigation. I'd wager that all save a very few have left this place already."

"You are right," I said. "But there were some few who made their names accursed and shunned among our people. Will *they* dare the ways of Antri, with their master overthrown?"

"Is he overthrown?" asked my father, with a quizzical air. "I had some such notion, but it was blasted from my foolish old head with the first of our friend's lightnings. Had the gods not sent Mowen to meet us on the mountain, we old fools would be motes upon the wind by now."

"He is overthrown," I said, and my words echoed through me in a surge of confidence. "The gods have set us all here—Harl from the far north, Zorek from Krel, Shal and Grem from our own hills, Mowen from Antri, and you and me, the last of Lantir. Not without reason do those cold beings take the trouble to move their pawns about the board."

"Perhaps," he said, "but look to the cooking before you ladle the soup."

I looked past him at the table where the Warlock stood —and met his eyes. The flickers died away, leaving a terrible quiet where that incessant tumult had clashed for so long. The Warlock straightened his hunched shoulders, his face pale and his eyes, I saw now, a burning red like that of the panels on the floor behind us. He stood upright and leveled his forefinger at me.

"*Ingharath!*" he shouted, and a shape made of shadow dropped from the darkness beneath the vaulted roof, straight toward me. But Harl growled deep in his throat and raised his blade, making a crossing motion with it.

"*Gaerl!*" he roared, and something struck the shadow and . . . ate it.

The Wizard paled, and his eyes seemed redder than ever. "*Alioish in haram nathi!*" he intoned, carefully. "*In haram nathoniahm.*"

A stiffness grew in my muscles. My bones seemed turned brittle and icy, and I felt my eyeballs begin to congeal in my skull. But Zorek was there, once again, now freed from his duties of turning aside the lightning. He touched my forehead with his right forefinger and muttered under his breath. At once, I breathed freely, and the deathlike feeling left me.

I laid my hand on his shoulder in thanks, then I stood forth from the rest and said, "Wizard, it seems that my comrades counter every spell you know. Let us once again leave the solution of our differences to fate. You won this kingdom with a roll of the dice. Are you willing to risk it upon another?"

His eyes narrowed, and I saw him considering every chance, every opening left to him, every deceit that he might yet use. Then he relaxed his tense shoulders a bit, though the tension did not leave the corners of his eyes and mouth.

"Yes," he said, and his voice was a distant twittering, instead of the bass rumble of old. "We will leave it to the gods." And he laughed long and soundlessly.

CHAPTER 15

An unspoken truce prevailed, for the while. Though he sought to avoid showing it, the Warlock was exhausted and withdrew to his own rooms, leaving us to find what comfort we could. Carrying Mowen, Harl led the way into the corridor, and my father pointed away to our right.

"The kitchens are there, through a cross-corridor," he said. "Come, this is the way we came." And he strode ahead of Harl, and we all followed them.

The kitchens were large, fitted with tremendous hooks and caldrons that swung about the hearths. Fires still burned there, but the servants had gone away down the road after their betters. Only an old woman sat there alone, tears leaking slowly from her wrinkled eyelids to the corners of her mouth as she rubbed her cracked, warped hands slowly together in her lap.

"He'm gone, he'm gone and left uns," she mourned over and over.

I recognized her from the vision Varil had sent to me, and I leaned over her. "You are safe, Old One. And your son is not gone forever, I would say. He will be back, when word goes out, for looting is a thing to his liking, from the sound of him. Will you show us a cupboard with dishes, that we may get ourselves some soup from this pot?"

She looked up at me, her eyes dim with webbing of white over their irises. "You'm hungry?" she whispered, and I nodded. "M'm get you food. M'm like to give folk food . . . they'm 'nt let me since m'm can't see so, now." She rose and shuffled to a wide-doored shelf and fumbled about, bringing out thick crockery bowls and the handled cups that were newly come to our backward land. Spoons appeared from a drawer, and she set them carefully on the table with the cups.

The stew in the pot, while certainly meant for the servants' meal, was fit for any king who ever walked, being thick with meat and dried vegetables. Into the cups she poured herb teas, and we were warmed and comforted by both the warmth and the content of the food and drink. The old woman would not sit with us but ate, nevertheless, from the top of a low chest, mumbling all the while her toothless murmur.

When we had eaten and rested, we looked outside, to find both moons in a clear sky, Ralias far down in the west, To-Sen almost overhead. I turned to my father and caught him to me, for one moment.

"There is light enough for traveling. Though I know that you and Grom and Mowen are weary beyond measure, you must go now, down that smooth road that leads all the way to Antri. With Harl and Zorek and Shal and Grem to aid you, you should come there in safety and fairly soon. I would that those I love and value were beyond the reach of danger, when the time comes that I roll dice with the Warlock."

"None will go," he answered, looking me squarely in the eyes. "My fault brought us all here into this peril. I, at least, will remain and see the game ended, let the dice roll as they may. Though I wonder . . . why did you think to leave it to that?"

I shook my head and did not answer. Turning to Grem, I said, "Your father needs you, my friend. Go to him, down in the hills, and help to gather your people again into a community." But he shook his head, wordlessly.

Shal forestalled me, saying, "Remi and my children are well enough. Even should I die here by your side, she would not want, for she is as skilled and as strong as I, capable more than most. She would disown me, should I leave you now."

Harl crossed his hands on his sword hilt and looked me in the eyes, and I knew his answer, as well as Grom's, who stood beside him. I looked at Mowen, who now, after food and rest, stood straight and strong again.

"I am sent here by the gods," she said, simply, "and I cannot leave until they give me a sign that I must. And now I have a colleague, things will not again go so ill as they did before when I stood alone."

She laid her hand on Zorek's shoulder and asked him, "How is it, Mercenary, that you know the secrets that we thought were taught only by Him Who Calls Upon the Name?"

Zorek smiled, rather bleakly. "I was not always nor solely a mercenary, Lady. Once I was a priest in just such a House as that which trained you and your brothers and sisters. It was not here, nor was it in Krel, but far at the edge of another ocean than the blue one that laps the beaches of Krel. I was trained beside the Purple Waters in a Temple much like those here. And I was further trained, when I left my place to wander, as a youth will, by the Initiates in the Towers of Truth, who dwell even farther away. Becoming a mercenary was a matter of unwisdom and ill-luck and the headstrong passions of being young. Would that I were still unstained by self-interest, as you are."

I looked them over, one by one, knowing that each was as steadfast as I was myself, and said: "Then if none will go to safety, then promise me one thing. When I call out to you, flee quickly beyond the confines of the Citadel. It may be that this stone shell will crumble beneath pressures it was not built to withstand. I welcome you into this contest, for I fully expect that the Warlock will not lose, if lose he does, in a gentlemanly manner. I will need eyes at my back and to both sides."

We rested, then, once more, though none of us could sleep beneath that dire roof. And when the sun rose, we ate the food that the old woman cooked for us, stretched the stiffness from our bones, and went again up that curving corridor to the door of the Warlock's sanctum. Hearing a shuffle behind us, I looked back to see the old woman coming along behind, mumbling toothlessly all the while.

We passed the crumbled doors and found the chamber beyond alight with lamps hung from hoops that swung from the roof. The Warlock was waiting, his face less pale and his eyes less red than they had been when last we saw him. On the table before him was an ivory cup and a set of dice, together with a ruby-colored flagon of wine and nine cups.

"You are punctual," he said, his voice more nearly that which I remembered. "It is well. Come and drink with me before we toss our fateful throws at the feet of the gods."

He poured the cups full, leaving the flagon empty, and took a cup into his own hand. We came forward in a body and took up the others, lifting them to one another. Then I turned the cup in my hand and poured the contents out on the floor. Zorek followed suit, and my father and all the rest of them.

He gasped, and I turned to him and said in a voice of angelic sweetness, "Who drinks with a wizard does well to down an empty cup." His face regained something of that whiteness of the night before, but he said nothing, just gestured toward the dice and the dice cup.

"Yours be the first cast," I said. "As you provide the dice, I will name the toss. The low man wins all, one throw out of two. Pray to your demons, wizard, for I will pray to the gods."

He was deadly pale, now, and his eyes had kindled again, burning red in the lamplight. He took up the cup and tossed into it the dice, gazing long at them as if musing. Then he threw. And a one and a two came up.

I laughed. "A difficult toss to beat, Warlock. But I shall try, even as you did, to make that come to pass."

I cupped the dice, but I needed no gazing at them to make them do my will. I had hurled boulders with pinpoint accuracy. Two fragments of jewelstone were nothing.

I rattled them in the cup and tossed. One and one glittered up at us like the eyes of a serpent.

The Warlock made a choked sound, and I found myself facing the two slabs of red stone that had been in the door. He stood before them, seeming to draw forth from them some energy. But before he could complete his intention, my father walked about the table and made again the symbol of Riha on the smooth stone.

"I give you blessing . . . and peace," he said, and the glow died away, leaving the stones dead and almost colorless.

Then, from the door that must have led to his own chamber, the Warlock called out a dozen armed men, who came at us with closed helms and bared blades. We drew our swords from their slings and made ready for battle. But Mowen, looking closely at the incomers, began to chant, and Zorek, with a start of surprise, took it up with her.

We watched, unbelieving, as the flesh of the warriors lost its substance, dissolving away like dew in the morning sun. Before they came within blade's reach of us, they were gone, and empty breastplates and helms and armlets clattered to the floor.

His eyes blazing, the Warlock reached blindly behind him and drew forth a rounded jewel that sparked wickedly in the brightness of the room. He held it out toward us, and immediately a thin keening filled my ears and my whole mind, blurring all thought and volition. About me, my comrades were clutching their hands to their ears and moaning, though I was only dimly aware of it.

As I fought to regain my senses fully, I saw a strange little figure shuffle past me, moving toward the Warlock. As it went it mumbled, "Bad boy, you'm burn m'self. Come, gi't't Alli. Boy'm not let to play wi' such."

Fires crackled about her grizzled head, but she seemed to notice nothing as she faced the dumbfounded Warlock and took the stone from his hand. She looked down at it indifferently, then dropped it onto the floor and ground it under her heel, making a blaze of sparks and crackles.

"Uns dangerous!" she admonished. "Wicked things 'm be put away!" Then, glowing from within as if she were a newly kindled lamp, she opened her webbed eyes wide, said, "M'm goin'!" and crumpled out of sight behind the table.

Empty-handed, the Warlock drew a deep breath and began a chant so ominous that I knew the time had come. Crying, "Out, for your lives!" I pulled inward against the buttressed weight of the arched roof, striving with all my might to loose the keystone from its position. The thing groaned, I felt a shifting. Trusting to my companions to run from the spot, I pulled the roof inward, leaping backward, as I did so, into the low-ceiled corridor. A rumbling and crashing and a thunder of fallen masonry sounded, and I turned and ran for my own life, out through the kitchen corridor, out of the back door that now stood wide.

The Citadel did not crumble outward. It fell into itself as if it were a flower un-blooming itself, curling back into a bud. I stood in the stableyard, again left to the geese and chickens, and watched the Warlock's keep diminish into a low pile of rubble. A hand on my shoulder made me turn to find my father behind me, with the rest of our group.

He looked past me at the ruin and said, "I have lived all my life in the hands of the gods, but only now am I truly aware of it. Each one of us was here with a mission only he could fulfill, and each of us stood the test. Even the poor old woman Alli had her task to do, and she did it nobly."

"It is true," I replied. "Yet . . . it seems a pity. I found proof, deep in the caverns under the plain, that the Warlock's forefathers were here long before our own folk ever came down from the north. They were leaders of men, though they practiced foul arts. In some way, he may have had a right to rule here."

"If so, he had his opportunity, and he failed his own test," my father said sternly. "Let it be—the gods have spoken last of all." And he turned away toward Antri.

CHAPTER 16

So it came about that my father again rules in Lantirion. And I am again a prince, though a far better one than I might have been, lacking the rigors of the past years.

I sit before another hearthfire—my own, and Varil smiles at me from its other side, her lap full of charts and tables that make no sense at all to me. She is now Princess Royal of Lantirion, Keeper of the Truth, and Associate of Him Who Calls Upon the Name. Her sorceries have been proclaimed officially, and without any question, of the purest and most beneficial kind, used solely for the good of her land and its people.

Any who dared to question her suitability as next Queen of Lantirion would find himself stoned from the streets of Antri, from the plains, and from the hills. As well as attacked and mauled by our three sons and two daughters, all of whom combine her wits with my own physical endowments. And all of whom are learning to cheat at games of toss-stones and marbles, with the aid of a certain talent inherited from their father.

I am not idle. We have an army, small but the equal of many that are bigger and better armed. My commander is a certain Zorek, who is also an associate of the Temple, on intimate terms with Him Who Calls Upon the Name. I think it not unlikely that he and Mowen will wed, when her full time of training is ended, though it has meant a wait of many years on their part. Hopeful I am that they will not be too old to provide heirs of their house, that my own younglings will have such friends as I possess.

It did not surprise me that Renath ended her long widowhood, taking Harl into the warmth of her home, together with a score of orphaned children. They did not return to the plain but stayed behind in the hills to aid Adalla, and on her death they became the unofficial leaders of both hill and plain. I was pleased at this final welding together of the two folk, both so worthy, yet for long so divided. With Shal and Grem, they make up the council that decides issues in the hills.

Grom has gone back to his native earth, though I still hear his gravelly voice, at times, when I am hunting in the hills or counting sheep out on the plains with my heirs. I teach them as he taught me, to take interest in everything, great or small, that comes about in our lands. We travel together over all the ways that I went, on my long adventure, and I tell them the tale again and again.

We have never sought out the caverns through which I wandered. I wish never again to come into that buried Temple with its horrible instruments and its unburied dead. But we did find the bones of my horse, scattered and few after so many years, and I recounted to them my battle with the quall. And they never fail to shiver when I tell them of the wind that their mother sent through that cleft to sweep the beasts to their doom.

Ours is no perfect land of total harmony and utter peace. Twice we have had rumblings from the Krel to the north, and once we fought a small but fierce battle at the northern juncture of our two mountain chains, stopping a probing army in its tracks.

There are squabblings and mutterings among high and low, as there have ever been, and will ever be. But we keep a finely honed ear to such, and we never allow them to grow into disagreements that sprout factions. The few of the Warlock's henchmen who went to earth so well that we were unable to find them send up little bubblings of unrest, now and again, but they are so well shunned that they make no worry for us.

And the Citadel that stood so proudly on the shoulder of Fire-Shouter is now a place where families jaunt, in summer, over that smooth road that leads to it from Antri. They sit and eat their lunches in the stableyard and point to the stone we placed for old Alli. It reads: *Here, under the stones of the Citadel, lies Alli, mother of Ahoris, who died in service to the gods.*

We set no stone for the Warlock.

Our winters are milder, now, and the snows are no more than enough to set a good season in the soil. May the gods grant that we never again see such a winter as was the last gift of the Warlock!